D1650035

SPECIAL MESSAGE TO READERS

THE ULVERSCROFT FOUNDATION
(registered UK charity number 264873)
was established in 1972 to provide funds for
research, diagnosis and treatment of eye diseases.
Examples of major projects funded by
the Ulverscroft Foundation are:-

- The Children's Eye Unit at Moorfields Eye Hospital, London
- The Ulverscroft Children's Eye Unit at Great Ormond Street Hospital for Sick Children
- Funding research into eye diseases and treatment at the Department of Ophthalmology, University of Leicester
- The Ulverscroft Vision Research Group, Institute of Child Health
- Twin operating theatres at the Western Ophthalmic Hospital, London
- The Chair of Ophthalmology at the Royal Australian College of Ophthalmologists

You can help further the work of the Foundation
by making a donation or leaving a legacy.
Every contribution is gratefully received. If you
would like to help support the Foundation or
require further information, please contact:

THE ULVERSCROFT FOUNDATION
The Green, Bradgate Road, Anstey
Leicester LE7 7FU, England
Tel: (0116) 236 4325

website: www.foundation.ulverscroft.com

HEART OF THE MOUNTAIN

Emotionally burned out from her job as a nurse, Beth leaves London for the Scottish Highlands and the peace of her aunt's cottage. Here she meets Alex, a man who is determined to live life to the full after the death of his fiancée in a climbing accident. Despite her wish for a quiet life, Beth is pulled into a friendship with Alex's sister, bubbly Sarah-Jayne, and finds herself increasingly drawn to Alex . . .

CAROL MacLEAN

HEART OF THE MOUNTAIN

Complete and Unabridged

LINFORD
Leicester

First published in Great Britain in 2016

First Linford Edition
published 2017

Copyright © 2016 by Carol MacLean

*A catalogue record for this book is available
from the British Library.*

ISBN 978–1–4448–3221–1

Published by
F. A. Thorpe (Publishing)
Anstey, Leicestershire

Set by Words & Graphics Ltd.
Anstey, Leicestershire
Printed and bound in Great Britain by
T. J. International Ltd., Padstow, Cornwall

This book is printed on acid-free paper

1

The coffee was mediocre but the cafe was clean and the staff cheerful. Beth Hainshaw asked for a refill anyway. She needed the caffeine kick. She sipped the brew as she stared out of the window at the windblown hedge and the motorway with its constant streak of cars. No doubt the window was double-glazed; thankfully she couldn't hear the noise and grind of the traffic.

She'd started her journey from London the morning before, and had spent the night in a pleasant bed-and-breakfast place in Berwick-upon-Tweed. All day driving north up the busy motorways, with only her car radio for company. Now, flicking a glance at her wristwatch, she guessed she had at least another couple of hours before she reached her destination. Her handbag buzzed and she rummaged for her phone. Her mother's number.

Before she answered, Beth took a deep gulp of the coffee.

'Is that you, Beth?'

As if it was going to be anyone else answering her phone.

'Mum, how are you? Everything alright?'

'Speak up, dear, I can hardly hear you. Where are you? Are you still in England?'

'No, I'm at a rest stop having lunch. I crossed the border into Scotland a few hours ago.'

There had been a huge blue sign at the border, with the white cross of the Scottish flag, 'Welcome to Scotland' in huge letters and underneath, in the Gaelic, *'Failte gu Alba'*. She supposed that meant the same. Despite herself, she'd felt a ripple of excitement at the foreign language on the board. A sense of reaching new land.

Then she'd been sadly disappointed to discover that the Scotland she was driving through looked very much like the English countryside she'd passed by for hours. However, the landscape was

2

changing now. The low rolling hills and fertile farms had gone and instead the countryside had a rougher look, with willow scrub and wild grass, and in the distance much higher mountain peaks.

'I've never been to Scotland,' her mother said. 'I never saw the need for it.'

'No, well …' Beth tailed off. It was hard to explain why she was here.

'I don't understand why Moira lent you her cottage. It's not as if you're properly ill, is it?'

'No, I suppose not,' Beth said. Her head was beginning to ache, just at her temples. She was sure some of her colleagues had felt the same way about her time off work, although her close friends had been kind and supportive.

'I mean, *stress* is a modern ailment. We didn't have *stress* when I was young. We just got on with life. We were tougher back then. You young people don't know how good you've got it.'

Beth let the words flow over her and tried not to mind. She hadn't fully understood her own illness until her GP had explained that no, she couldn't keep working on through it, and yes, she had to fully relax and let her mind and body heal. Dr O'Neill had signed her off work with a determined flourish of his pen and a firm stare. She had got the message.

'I blame Moira for this,' Milly Hainshaw went on, her voice sharp and tinny on Beth's old phone. 'If she hadn't offered you the use of her holiday home, you wouldn't have given up your job.'

'That's not true, Mum. It was very kind of Auntie Moira to let me use the cottage for a few weeks. That's not why I handed in my notice.'

Her mother's older sister had a number of properties, courtesy of her rich second husband, most of which were strategically placed to follow the sun. Moira and Jonathon were currently in San Sebastian enjoying an average of thirty degrees Celsius, which suited their health. They hardly ever used the Scottish property, she told Beth, and she was welcome to stay as long as she liked.

'What on earth possessed you to do so,

then? It's so … *reckless*. So unlike you, Beth. You're usually sensible.'

'I need some time away. It's not a disaster. I need to think about my future, about what I want to do next. And if it comes to it, I can always get agency nursing when I'm up to working again.'

'I know you were upset when Lisa passed away, but I don't understand what was different. You're a hospice nurse, you must be used to losing your patients.'

The waitress came across to take away Beth's empty cup and the remains of her cheese and pickle sandwich. She wiped the table and laid out cutlery and paper napkin as if Beth was going to ask for a second meal. Beth smiled politely. The cafe was filling up with another round of hungry travellers looking for lunch, and they needed her table.

'I've got to go, Mum. I'll call you later. Let you know that I got there safely.'

She pressed the red button on her phone before her mother could reply. She'd text later. A quick message. She wasn't up for another conversation with

5

her parent today. Somehow, she always came away emotionally drained.

In the car, she checked the map she'd printed out. The blue line from London to the tiny village of Invermalloch in the Scottish Highlands looked simple and direct. But turning the page, she saw the final stage of her journey was via a network of single-track roads with sparse settlements dotted about. The last reasonably sized town was Fort William. Perhaps she'd stop there for a snack before she headed into the wilderness.

Was there a shop in Invermalloch? Was the cottage stocked with food? Or should she find a supermarket in Fort William and buy masses of tins and cartons just in case? Her stomach clenched all of a sudden. Her mother was right. What on earth was she doing? She'd packed up her familiar life in London abruptly. Let her flat out to rent, said goodbye to her good friends and handed in her notice for a job she'd done efficiently for ten years, and enjoyed — right up until a year ago.

There was no going back. Not yet, at

any rate. Moira was right. She needed at least a few weeks, maybe longer, to recover and to find out what she wanted to do with the rest of her life. Thank goodness for her aunt. She understood Beth, much more than her own mother did.

*   *   *

Beth smiled. End Cottage had been named by someone with either a distinct lack of imagination or a very dry sense of humour. It literally was the last house in the village. The end cottage in a row of three low, whitewashed houses, before the marsh and tussocky purple heather claimed the land once more.

She slipped the key from her pocket and flexed her shoulders. Her muscles ached from sitting in her car for two days and she was suddenly glad to be standing there, free from driving and ready for the next phase of her life to begin. She unlocked the blue painted door and pushed it open. The scent of lavender wax polish and cold air wafted towards her.

The little house was pristine clean and, despite the ancient exterior, very modern inside. Moira had high standards.

She drifted through the kitchen, admiring the gleaming cooker, large dishwasher and complex-looking washing machine. She could hardly imagine Moira and Jonathon requiring the machines on their brief visits. The place was like a show room, except for one dripping tap at the sink. The living room was comfortable, with a suite of olive green velvet and wood armchairs and sofa and matching green drapes. No television, Beth noted, and was pleased. She didn't want the intrusion of the world and all its harshness into her new little house. Not yet. She wasn't ready for it.

She climbed the narrow, crooked staircase to find two small bedrooms and a reasonably sized bathroom. Then, her exploration of End Cottage finished, she went back to the kitchen to make coffee. She sent a silent thank you to Moira as she pulled open a cupboard to discover a silver cafetiere and a pretty set of china mugs. End Cottage was simply perfect.

'Coffee, coffee ... where in the car will the coffee be?' she murmured, thinking of her shopping trip to the supermarket on the way to the village. She'd bought enough to survive a siege, not knowing what kind of shops Invermalloch might offer. Lifting the cafetiere onto the work-top she stopped. Someone had left a basket lined with a paper doily and filled with various items. She hadn't noticed it before, she'd been so impressed with the layout of the kitchen. There was a small bag of filter coffee along with a handful of creamers, the kind that hotels usually leave out. In fact, it looked as if whoever had left it had raided a hotel for the rest too. There were miniature glass jars of jams, butter in gold foil and finally a wrapped chocolate.

'Coffee first, questions later,' Beth told herself, filling the kettle and flicking the switch.

There was peace in carrying out the mundane actions. While making food or drink, cleaning her house or shopping,

Beth didn't need to think. It was only when she stopped that the thoughts began.

She took her coffee outside to the back garden. It was low maintenance, just mown grass and a few shrubs. Her mother's words came back to her. *Reckless.* Was she being reckless? It didn't feel like it. It felt like … like she had come home. There was a calmness here that called to her. She felt safe. She could imagine living in End Cottage, at least for a while. Until she was better. Because despite what Milly Hainshaw believed, Beth wasn't well. She was recovering but there was a way to go yet. She knew that. Lisa's death had hit her hard. As a hospice nurse she knew — of course she knew — that no matter how much she cared for her patients, they were not going to get better. She had been taught how to keep an emotional distance. It was important to be gentle and kind and give the best care possible, but it was vital to not get emotionally involved. There was a percentage burn out of nurses and Beth had vowed not to be one of them.

In the end, that had proved impossible. Lisa was sixteen when she came to the hospice. A bright, funny girl with a gift of making people laugh. Beth had been drawn to her. Lisa had loved to chat. Beth firmly believed that conversation was therapy too. Lisa had become like a younger sister to her. And watching her die slowly over the six months of their friendship had been agony.

Beth's manager had taken her aside and admonished her for getting too close to Lisa. She was to retain her professionalism, Sister McLaren had told her sternly. But there was sympathy in her eyes as she spoke.

Beth sighed. She drank the last dregs of her coffee and set the cup down on a spindly iron table that stood crookedly on the uneven grass. With an effort she put her shoulders back and stood up straight. She took a deep breath of the fresh mountain air and forced herself to relax.

'That's better. One day at a time, Bethany Hainshaw; that's all I ask.' The tears pricked behind her eyelids but she refused to let them fall. She could do this. *She could.* This was her fresh start.

'Get the shopping in first. Put it all away in those cute, dinky little cupboards and then think about what's for dinner.' The sound of her own voice was daft but comforting. She forced a smile. *Much better.* A blackbird landed on the grass, cocking its head to peer at her.

'I don't have any food for you just now. But if you come back in a while, I might have found the loaf of bread,' she told it, and then felt foolish for talking to an animal. Perhaps she'd buy a bird feeder. She could place it in front of the kitchen window. Something to watch. Something to distract her from …

'Ms Hainshaw?' A deep voice, polite but with more than a hint of reserve. Beth spun round, her heart running a little faster. She hadn't expected company. A tall, dark-haired man stood on the path running beside her cottage and the next one.

'Yes?' Beth felt a rush of

embarrassment. Had he heard her talking to herself? *Worse still, talking to a bird.*

If he had heard her, he didn't say. He moved towards her, hand out to shake hers.

'I'm Alex. Alex Taylor. Moira's neighbour. She phoned me to say you'd be moving in here for a few months.'

His handshake was warm and strong. There was a pause between them. She was briefly annoyed at his interruption. Then he was speaking again.

'I came to fix the tap.' He pulled a spanner from his pocket as if to prove it.

'Oh.' Was that all she could come up with? Beth mentally kicked herself. It was a struggle to be sociable when all she really wanted was to be on her own.

He stood patiently. The blackbird sang its rickety song, safe in the apple tree at the corner of the garden. She noticed Alex's nose was slightly bent and decided it had been broken at some point in his past.

'So, may I?'
'Sorry?'

'May I fix your tap for you?' Slowly as if he was dealing with an idiot.

She flushed.

'Yes, yes of course. Please come in.' She led the way into the kitchen.

There wasn't much space with two of them in the room. She hung back, practically in the hallway, watching him hunker down to check the pipes under the sink. Then he stood and worked at the sink. Beth was left with the view of his broad back. He didn't appear to mind the silence and made no effort to chat while he dismantled the tap. She forced some energy for a conversation.

'Thank you for the coffee and creamers.' *First prize for inane chat, Beth.*

He glanced up, looking puzzled. She pointed to the basket. He nodded.

'Not me. My sister, Sarah-Jayne, left them for you.'

'That was nice of her. Does she live nearby too?'

'No, Sarah-Jayne lives on the other side of the burn but she's a real home-maker and she thought you'd like a welcome pack.'

'The burn?'

Alex turned the tap on and off with a flourish. The drip had stopped. He grinned at her and it made him look younger than she'd first guessed him to be. When he smiled, he looked about her own age, early thirties at most.

'A burn is a Scottish word for a stream,' he explained.

'Right. I knew that.' She smiled back, self-mocking.

He smiled at her again and it was if they had finally found a common ground. The beginning of understanding each other.

'I'm hearing London in your accent. It's not so different up here though. You'll soon settle in.'

'Will I?' The words spilled out before she could filter her brain.

'It depends on why you came here. This place is great for outdoor activities. If you like hill walking, climbing or fishing then you're in for a treat. If you like theatre and shopping, not so good.'

'Are you the maintenance man for

the cottage?' Beth asked, switching the subject. The idea of crazy sports pursuits had her shuddering inside. Not what the doctor had ordered, not at all.

'No, there is a regular handyman but he's not about today so I'm doing this as a favour to Moira. She wanted to you to arrive somewhere comfortable with all in order. I'm a climbing instructor.'

That figured. He had a muscled build like he worked out a lot. Maybe that explained the broken nose too.

'Sounds risky.'

He touched a finger to his nose and smiled. 'This wasn't a climbing accident. My nose got broken a lifetime ago. Climbing isn't too risky if you know what you're doing. I run wildlife tours too, if you're ever interested in seeing the local area.'

He'd read her mind uncannily on the issue of his nose. Then she was absurdly disappointed with him. It was a sales pitch. However friendly he sounded. What did she care anyway? Wasn't solitude what she craved?

16

'I won't have time.' Warmth infused her neck. She was being rude and knew it. But she didn't like pushy. Didn't want to be corralled into going on one of his tours out of politeness. She laced her knuckles, feeling the bones grate painfully together.

'I understand. You're busy,' he glanced about, as if trying to figure out in which way she could possibly be so busy. 'What is it you do?'

'I'm a nurse ...' She halted, then said honestly, 'I *was* a nurse.'

He didn't ask. He picked up the spanner, gave the top of the tap a last tighten and stuck the tool in his pocket. With a slight nod he headed out the back door and made a turn onto the side path. Beth followed him out. Just to make sure he was actually leaving, she thought. He hesitated and looked back at her.

'I'll ask Sarah-Jayne to pop in on you. She's very sociable, she'll be glad to meet you.'

'Oh, no — really, you don't have to.' *Please don't.* 'I wouldn't like to put her out.'

His gaze caught hers and she had the extraordinary and fleeting impression that he could see right into her soul.

'It's no bother. To be honest, she's a bit lonely with her husband away. I think it'd be good for her too.'

With a slight wave, he was gone. And Beth was left to ponder his words. It'd be good for her *too*. Implying that Beth was lonely. Well, he was wrong there. She wasn't lonely. But she definitely did want to be alone. She could only hope that Alex Taylor was her last visitor to End Cottage.

2

Alex's mouth twisted wryly. His new neighbour was as prickly as a cat whose fur was brushed up the wrong way.

'I don't mean a cat like you,' he told Tony, who yawned and jumped down from the stairs to offer a lazy welcome home. 'You quite like your fur rubbed tail to ears, don't you, old fellow?'

Beth Hainshaw had an aura of sadness. Without spelling it out, she'd made it clear he was intruding into her personal space. While fixing her dripping tap, he'd got the strong vibe that he wasn't wanted there. He shrugged. He was helping Moira. If Ms Hainshaw didn't want his company that was fine by him. He'd only suggested the wildlife tours because she looked out of place in the cottage, dressed in her London fashions with her glossy black hair neatly bobbed. He wasn't good with hair styles but he'd bet it cost more than he spent on a week's groceries. She looked what she was, a city girl far from home. The offer of the tour had been spontaneous. It would get her out and about, let her view the country. Instead of being grateful, she'd been affronted.

'Is it fair to set my sister on to her?' he asked Tony. 'You know Sarah-Jayne, she loves a challenge and she loves company.'

Tony purred and tried to lead Alex to his food bowl.

'Later, cat. Now I've got to pick up Bryn and get to the Post.'

He left a disappointed feline, picked up his car keys and drove off towards the modern housing estate where Bryn lived. For some reason his mind was still on his new neighbour. He'd ring Sarah-Jayne later and ask her to call in at End Cottage. Goodness knows, his sister had her own problems. It might just help both women, finding a new friend.

* * *

Bryn welcomed him in. Alex and Bryn were both in the local Mountain Rescue Team and good friends. There had been a dramatic rescue of two young men on a high mountain just the day before, and an extra scare when Alex discovered a nick in his climbing rope.

Before he could discuss that, Bryn asked about the new occupant of End Cottage.

'What's she like? I bet she was grateful to get that tap mended. I know Moira wasn't happy about loaning the cottage in less than a perfect state, was she.'

'She's ... nice.' Although truthfully, he wasn't sure about that. She hadn't liked him. She'd wanted him gone. That wasn't 'nice'. So what was she? Lonely, scared, sad. All these descriptions fitted her. He didn't know why. And he wasn't going to share his impressions with Bryn. That wasn't fair to Beth Hainshaw. He should make up his own mind when he met her.

'Anyway, what happened with Darren?' Bryn said. 'Why didn't he fix the tap at End Cottage? I thought he was the handy man there.'

'He hasn't turned up the last while. Probably nursing a hangover,' Alex replied.

'Or avoiding you. There's a lot of history between you.'

'I'd like to think that's all in the past. He and I might not speak much, but I nod to him when I see him and he does too. All very amicable. No, I tend to think his drinking has got out of hand again. It's a wonder he manages to hold down all the maintenance jobs he's got round the village.'

'He's good at fixing things. That's how he holds on to contracts and odd jobs. If you can stand the man and his erratic hours then you'll get a good job done. Eventually.'

'Let's not waste more breath on Darren White,' Alex said. 'I came to give you a lift to the Post. I think we should go over the equipment.' After the cut rope, they had to check all the other ropes and climbing gear for any tampering or wear and tear.

'That was a good outcome yesterday

for that lad on the Buchaille. It could've gone completely differently. We were lucky.'

'Yes, it went well in the end. There was no real harm done.' Which was the truth, if you didn't count the lad's concussion and terror, and the cuts and bruises on Alex's back which were still painful.

The Mountain Rescue Post was situated in an old stone house which had once been the Manse. Inside it had been converted so that the rescue Land Rovers could drive straight in through double garage doors. There were two office rooms with telephones and computers and another large conference hall where the team met for talks and demonstrations. At the back of the conference hall were large cupboards where the communal gear was stored. Many of the volunteers brought their own ropes and rucksacks but some, like Alex, preferred to use the team equipment.

'I wonder how long Beth will be staying in the village,' Alex pondered. 'We could do with a nurse on the team.'

Bryn stared at him as if he'd grown

an extra head. 'She made quite an impression on you, didn't she? If I didn't know you better, I'd say she *interested* you.'

'And you'd be wrong,' Alex said, tersely.

'Am I? It's okay to like her, you know. It's better than okay. It's good, Alex.'

'It's not like that.'

'Isn't it?' Bryn said, gently. 'It's been five years, my friend. Gillian would want you to move on.'

Alex held up his hand, palm out. 'Don't.'

But Bryn persisted. 'She was my little sister. I loved her too. But she's gone and she's not coming back. If there's one thing I know about Gillian, it's that she would not want us to spend the rest of our lives in mourning for her. You have to move on. Find someone new.'

'I will never find someone to replace Gillian. Not ever,' Alex said. 'My heart belongs to her; it's as simple as that.' His tone brooked no reply.

They worked in silence for a while,

each searching methodically along the lengths of bright neon nylon climbing ropes without finding cuts or anything suspicious. They moved on to checking the hexes and harnesses.

'Nothing,' Bryn said finally.

'No,' Alex agreed.

'Do you honestly think someone tampered with that rope?' Bryn asked.

Alex shook his head. 'When I was up there, on that knife edge, yes. Definitely. But now, here in the Post with no evidence, no I don't. There was a cut in the rope. No doubt about that. But maybe it was wear and tear. I don't know. Every sense is heightened up there, you know that, Bryn. There is nothing keener than being on a rock face with nothing between you and God's green earth other than a single rope.'

'So, what now? We forget it?'

'Yes, we forget it. Put it down to misfortune, if you like.'

Bryn nodded. 'Okay, let's get the gear stashed away. You were lucky up there yesterday. We shouldn't forget that. I'm thinking extra practice this week for the team on rope techniques. You want to lead on that?'

'No, you lead it. Clearly I still have some stuff to learn.'

Bryn laughed and Alex was glad to hear his friend happy once more. But the echoes of their conversation stayed with him as he drove home. Bryn was wrong. Gillian wouldn't want him to forget her so easily. Besides which, his heart was locked and sealed. He would never open it up to anyone. The pain was too intense to bear a second time around.

★ ★ ★

'You must like chocolate cake.'

Sarah-Jayne wore cut-off jeans and a bright orange singlet. Her hair was a mass of copper curls and her legs were adorned with two toddlers, one on either side. They clung to her, sucking on dummies, half-naked in only nappies and stained tee-shirts. A third child, slightly older, raced around Beth's small living room,

26

knocking over cushions and ornaments with abandon.

Beth was momentarily speechless. She'd spent the morning unpacking, having been too tired the previous evening to bother. The doorbell ringing had been an unwelcome interruption. At first she thought it must be the postman bringing sales leaflets and other junk. When she opened the door, a chocolate cake was thrust in her face. Without asking, the woman had followed her inside, shutting the door behind her.

'Everyone likes it. That's a scientific fact. So, where does Moira keep her plates?' Sarah-Jayne didn't wait for an answer but drifted through to Beth's kitchen and opened cupboard doors 'til she found what she was looking for. 'What size slice to do you want? Personally, I like a good-sized piece. No point otherwise. Jade! Stop that. Come get some cake. Skye and Peri, you can have a wee bit, but not too much, okay.'

Beth was seated at her own wooden table with a plate of home-made cake in front of her before she could draw breath. Across from her, Sarah-Jayne grinned and waved a fork, scattering cake crumbs.

'Good, eh? That's my granny's recipe. There's a secret ingredient. Don't ask, 'cos I'm not telling.'

'I wouldn't dream of it,' Beth said faintly. She took up her fork and scooped up some cake. It was divine. She began to warm to Sarah-Jayne. A woman who made such good cake couldn't be all bad. Even if she had disrupted Beth's precious peace.

'You're Moira's niece.' A statement.

Beth nodded. She swallowed her cake. Despite her desire to be on her own, she suddenly felt it would be rude not to offer her guest a drink.

'Tea or coffee?'

Sarah-Jayne looked ridiculously pleased. 'Tea, please. Have you got herbal?'

'I don't think so,' Beth said apologetically. 'I've got normal tea.'

'That's really unhealthy. You should only drink herbals, like peppermint or blackberry. I'll bring you some next time.'

Next time. Beth felt her personal space shrink rapidly. She ought to put this woman off. Now. Forever. Instead, she heard herself say, 'Okay, that'd be nice. Thanks.'

'More cake?' Sarah-Jayne didn't wait for an answer. She scooped up a huge slice and landed it on Beth's plate. 'So, you've met my brother Alex. What do you think? Bit of a lost cause, eh?'

Beth was taken aback by her visitor's honesty. 'He seemed ... nice.'

'Nice?' Sarah-Jayne mocked. 'Alex isn't *nice*. He's complicated and annoying and repressed. But he isn't nice.'

'He wasn't here for long,' Beth said. 'He fixed my tap and left.' She didn't add that she had willed him to leave with all her might.

'He fixed your tap? Weird. I thought Darren did the maintenance here.' Sarah-Jayne brightened. 'Hey, have you met Darren? Don't you think he looks like a movie star?'

'No, I haven't met him. Aren't you married?' Beth tried, and failed, to keep the disapproval from her voice. She was sure Alex had said his sister was married. Clearly she had some kind of relationship, past or present, given she had three children.

'Yes, Andrew is working abroad for the next few months. I'm stuck with three kids and it's all a bit of a nightmare really. Do you want children?'

'I ... haven't given it much thought,' Beth lied. She had wanted children. Wanted to fall in love and get married and have a family. But that was before Lisa died. Her life had changed. Now she couldn't imagine having enough *heart* to do so. Lisa's death had shown her how difficult it was to love someone and to let them go. She never wanted to put herself in that position.

'Really? I always wanted kids,' Sarah-Jayne chatted on. 'I got pregnant fast, that's why we got married. And it was only a few months after I'd had Jade that I fell for the twins. Andrew was angry with me when he found out I was expecting again. But it takes two to tango, doesn't it.

I think he's glad to have gone to America for a break.' Her voice tailed off.

Beth felt a surge of unexpected sympathy. 'I'm sure he loves them just as much as you do.'

'Of course he does!' Sarah-Jayne frowned. 'He's a great daddy,' she said, defensively.

'Yes, of course. Sorry.'

'*I'm* sorry. It's not your fault. So, where was I? Do you know, I've just had the greatest idea ever.' She paused for effect. Her twins gazed up at her, slack-mouthed. Jade, the oldest, ran circles without stopping.

'And that is?' Beth asked cautiously.

'I'm going to have a party for you. A meet-the-neighbour sort of thing. It'll be fab. What do you say?'

'Marvellous,' Beth mumbled. Inside, she cursed Alex Taylor for letting his sister loose on her. She owed him one. Big time.

3

A bottle of good French wine, wrapped in pink tissue paper, waited on the hall chair. Beside it, a bouquet of flowers; purple irises, white roses and sweet-scented lilac. There was no way Beth was taking a shop-bought cake to Sarah-Jayne's party.

Upstairs, she applied her make-up with a slightly shaking hand. Her chest felt tight with nerves. She was kicking herself for agreeing to go to what Sarah-Jayne had described as a small, informal gathering. It was the last thing she wanted. She thought of her living room sofa with longing. Oh, to be able to just curl up on that sofa with a glass of wine and a novel, instead! She sighed and stood back from the mirror to see the effect.

Her grey eyes were enormous and there were lines of strain around her lipsticked mouth. She moved her jaw, trying to ease her tension.

'You're being ridiculous. It's a party. You go, stay for an hour, greet the village and make your excuses,' she told her reflection, sharply.

Would Alex Taylor be there? The question popped into her head, uninvited. She sort of hoped he would be. She owed him an apology. She had come across as rude when they met, she was sure of it. She wanted him to know that wasn't the real her.

'But who is the real me?' The mirror Beth had no answer.

Since Lisa's death and her absence from work due to stress, she had changed. It hadn't helped that her supervisor, Sister McLaren, hadn't wanted her back until Beth was fully recovered, and certain she'd be able to control her emotions around the patients at the hospice. And that, Beth could no longer guarantee. Which was why she had handed in her notice.

The old Beth had confidence. She put on a bright and cheerful face and socialised easily with patients and staff alike. The old Beth would have enjoyed

33

Sarah-Jayne's party. Would have looked forward to it. A chance to meet new people, have a laugh, eat delicious food and arrive home late.

She smoothed down her blue summer dress and wondered if it was appropriate. Was it too formal? The matching sandals had three-inch heels, and were her favourite footwear. Too much for a village get-together? She had no idea. Her hair was freshly conditioned and straightened, her makeup applied and there was no other reason to delay.

Her stomach twinged as she picked up the bottle of wine and the bunch of flowers. She'd been in End Cottage a whole week now and barely ventured out. She'd discovered a small village store five minutes walk away and had gone there to buy essentials such as milk and bread. But apart from speaking to the woman who ran the shop, she'd spoken to no one in seven days. Tonight was going to break that up.

★　★　★

It was a tumble-down farmhouse with a roof missing tiles and wood trims desperate for fresh paint. The grass grew without fear of a lawn mower and there were several outhouses that had gone to ruin. It was the right place though. Soft music and laughter filtered out of an open window on the air and the door was wide open. As Beth got out of her car, several children burst out yelling and ran off into the fields.

Her finger hovered over the doorbell but before she could press it, a man arrived behind her.

'Ms Hainshaw, good evening.'

'It's Beth, if I can call you Alex.' Her smile was genuine. It was a relief that she knew him, that they could walk in together to the maelstrom of chatter and bodies she imagined inside.

'Beth,' he nodded. 'I must say thank you. You've given Sarah-Jayne an excuse to hold a party. It's just what she needs to distract her.'

'Why should she need distraction?' Beth asked.

But he didn't answer as his sister came into view with open arms, bringing with her a blast of warm party air.

'Alex! Beth! You're here. Not only that, you came together. How lovely. Come on in, there's wine and soft drinks and loads of snacks. I'm putting out hot food later. Beth, you're the guest of honour, so you come with me. Alex can catch you up later.'

Sarah-Jayne was dressed in a long, rainbow tie-dyed skirt and white peasant blouse. Beth immediately felt over-dressed. Beth was pulled along with her and introduced to the many people that thronged the room. Her head buzzed from the names and faces and, as soon as the opportunity arose, she escaped to a quieter corner. Her respite did not last long.

'Beth, we need you over here,' Sarah-Jayne shouted, gesturing her over with vigorous arm movements. Beside her, Alex was shaking his head and glowering.

Self-consciously Beth moved through the room, murmuring polite 'excuse me's until she reached Sarah-Jayne and Alex.

'You've got to help,' Sarah-Jayne said dramatically, clutching at Beth's arm. 'Alex is injured. He's bleeding. Bryn told me you're a nurse. Can you tend to him?'

'This really isn't necessary,' Alex said, his mouth a thin line.

'Don't be mad,' his sister cried. 'You could die of an infection ... or ... I don't know what! At least let Beth have a look at the wounds. For me, Alex. Please?'

To Beth's gaze, Alex didn't look like a man about to die from his wounds. More likely to die from seething annoyance at his sibling. He gave a curt nod and Beth found herself in the upstairs bathroom while Alex peeled off his shirt. She winced when she saw his torso. There were three long, deep cuts, partly healed. One had opened up and was bleeding.

'These look painful. How did you do this?' As she spoke, Beth opened up the first aid kit Sarah-Jayne had given her. The kit was a jumble of plasters and bandages and a child's plastic toy. Still, there was enough in it for her to deal with

Alex's injuries.

'It's nothing, just a couple of grazes. I knocked into the rocks last week on a rescue.'

'And you didn't think to get these checked out then?'

'I was too busy getting the casualty to hospital. *He* had a severe concussion and a possible broken arm from crashing into the rock.'

'How awful. Is he alright?'

'Yeah, he was kept in for observation. The arm wasn't broken, just badly bruised and his concussion ended up not causing chronic damage.' Alex tensed as Beth applied cotton balls dipped in antiseptic to the long, open cut.

'This cut could've done with a couple of stitches but as long as you don't strain it, it's going to heal okay. If you continue to climb, it might well open up again. I'd advise you to rest for a couple of weeks …' Beth tailed off at the expression on Alex's face. 'But you're not going to follow my advice, are you?'

'Asking me not to move around, not

to climb, is like asking me not to eat and drink.'

'Can't you ask your friend Bryn to run your business for a few days?'

Alex gave a dry laugh. 'You have no idea how busy it gets in the tourist season up here. We had a bus-load of fifty Americans this week, all wanting to see the majestic red deer stag and the golden eagle. Thankfully we managed both. Tomorrow I'm leading a climb on Beinn Chaorach for a Japanese customer who's never climbed before. No ropes, it's not a massive hill, but it's strenuous exercise. After that, we've more Stateside visitors coming on their own tour bus to see the lochs and hills of Glencoe but they want local guides. I might get a chance to rest come the autumn, before the winter climbing begins.'

'You love it, I can hear that. But don't you worry about the risks?' Beth asked, rolling up the bandages into neat rolls and packing them into the first aid kit.

'The risks are part and parcel of the experience. If there was no risk, I wouldn't be interested.'

'I don't pretend to understand that. The way you describe the person you rescued last week, he's lucky to be alive. Where's the fun in risking your life? It sounds irresponsible to me. Don't you care if you die? What about your family? Sarah-Jayne for example. Isn't it selfish to risk it all and maybe cause them the pain of mourning you forever. Just for a sport.'

She'd hit a nerve. It showed in Alex's dark scowl. Beth took a physical step back.

'People make life choices. You might not agree with them, but that doesn't make them irresponsible, as you put it. My fiancée, Gillian, lived for her sport, for climbing. She was at her happiest out on a cliff facing the odds. It made her feel alive.'

Beth had a bad feeling. He was using the past tense. Even before he spoke again, she'd guessed where it was going.

'She died in a climbing accident on Ben Nevis five years ago.'

'I'm so sorry,' Beth whispered.

'But here's the thing. If she had the

chance to live her life over and avoid that fate, I know she'd make the same choices. Live the same life full of risk and adventure.'

'Hasn't her passing made you more careful in your sports?'

Alex shook his head. 'The opposite. I'm pushing the limits where I can. Since Gillian died, I've tried skydiving, technical ice-climbing, solo climbing without ropes. Because I discovered that life is very sweet and very short. We owe it to ourselves to pack every minute with adventure and discovery. I owe it to Gillian to make the most of what I've got left. Her time has gone but mine hasn't.'

'Are you so certain that's what she would have wanted?' Beth asked.

'Look at it this way. I don't have any dependents. Sarah-Jayne is my only family and she's got Andrew and the kids. I don't intend to get involved in another relationship now Gillian's gone. So I'm a free agent and I get to choose what I want to do with my life. Simple.'

Beth zipped up the neatly packed first

aid kit. She got the distinct impression she was being warned off by Alex. A tiny flicker of annoyance rose in her chest. There was no need for him to do so. She had no designs on him. He wasn't a man she'd be attracted to. They were poles apart in personality, likes and dislikes.

'Thank you for bandaging the cuts,' Alex said stiffly.

Beth inclined her head. She was too mad with him to speak. She got up and placed the kit on the bathroom shelf. Alex's voice halted her.

'We could do with a nurse on the Rescue Team. Would you consider it?'

Beth's voice was chilly. 'I don't think so.'

* * *

Alex followed Beth's ramrod-straight back down the stairs and knew he'd handled it badly. It wasn't her fault. It was Bryn's. For saying that Beth interested Alex. Bryn was wrong. But the notion had to be nipped in the bud right now.

Small villages like Invermalloch could grow large blossoms of gossip. He had no intention of providing any. It was important that Beth knew where he stood.

He almost bumped into Beth when she halted at the bottom of the stairs. When he saw why she'd stopped, he muttered under his breath. Sarah-Jayne was waltzing with a man with slicked back fair hair and cowboy blue eyes. Darren White. She was flushed and giggling and oblivious to the stares and raised eyebrows of her guests.

'Who is that?' Beth said.

'That is your maintenance man for End Cottage,' Alex said with a bite of sarcasm. 'The one and only Darren White.'

'The movie star.'

'What? Look, can you manoeuvre my sister out of the hallway while I deal with Darren?'

She flicked him a glance which mixed uncertainty with humour.

'Don't panic, I'm simply going to have a word with him. Outside. No brawling in the house, that's a promise.'

There was a hint of a smile tugging at the edge of her lips. Then she clearly decided she was still frosty with him and the smile disappeared. Which was a pity. It lit up her face and made her lose the sadness that floated like a mist around her.

'And .... action.' Alex nodded at the couple who were veering towards them.

He was impressed with how discreetly Beth managed Sarah-Jayne. One minute she was in Darren's arms, waltzing; the next, her arm had been looped with Beth's and the two women were walking into the back of the house like old friends. Which left Darren to Alex.

'Let's take a walk.' Alex let Darren hear the steel in his tone. It was a friendly enough suggestion but they both knew he had no choice.

'Alex!' Bryn warned, hurrying to them.

Alex waved him away. 'It's okay, I've got this. It's not going to get out of hand, is it Darren?'

'Whatever you say, Taylor,' Darren sneered. 'Let's take it outside.' He puffed up his chest but Alex knew there was not much will behind the posturing. It was like his school days all over again. Darren White was a bully but there was no substance to him.

They went outside. Alex was glad to note that the party continued inside. There would be no spectators.

'You don't dance with my sister. She's a married woman. Find someone else to bother.'

'She's a flirt. Besides, she likes me and I like her. The fact she's your sister just makes it sweeter.'

'Why, you ...' Alex took a step forward, his fists balled.

Darren flinched and turned to run, as Alex heard Beth cry out — when had she appeared? He'd thought she was inside with Sarah-Jayne. Alex knew his expression was thunderous. He also knew he was one hundred percent in control of himself. He was not a young kid in the schoolyard. Not any more.

'You were going to ...' Beth said, coming up beside him.

'Hit him? No, I wasn't,' Alex told her calmly. 'Sarah-Jayne and I come from a family where expressing our emotions was encouraged by my creative, artistic mother. You can see that my sister has taken after the Taylor traditions. So did I, up until I was a teenager. Then I learned it was better to control myself. You wondered about my broken nose. If you're interested, I'll tell you that story sometime.'

He brushed past her. It shouldn't hurt that she believed him capable of violence, but it did.

Inside, the party was winding down. It was after midnight and yet it wasn't quite dark. The summer solstice was only days away, and here in the far north the midnight sun ruled at least for a while. The counterbalance to that was the long, dark winter that autumn slid into and spring clawed out of.

'Bad news,' Bryn said, coming up to him.

'Is Sarah-Jayne okay?' he asked quickly.

'Yes, she's fine. She's in the kitchen,

there's a load of them making up pots of tea and cake to close the party with. No, it's not her. It's the team Land Rovers.'

Alex frowned. 'What about them?'

'Conor McBain phoned,' said Bryn; Connor was a volunteer from the Rescue Team. 'Someone's scored the paintwork on both of them.'

They shared a concerned glance. Scoring on one Land Rover could be put down to an unfortunate accident, perhaps a scrape against tree branches on a narrow single-track road. But both vehicles? It was very unlikely.

'What do you want to do?' Bryn asked.

'Nothing we can do at this late hour. I suggest we mull it over tomorrow.' When Bryn agreed, Alex hurried back outside. He wasn't sure why. Beth had her own transport, he wasn't going to offer her a lift home. But they'd parted on a cool note, and he wanted to make it right with her. Whatever vague idea he had though, he could forget it. He was just in time to see the flash of her blue dress as she slipped into her car and slammed the door. The red Yaris drove away fast and competently, leaving Alex standing on the farmhouse step alone.

4

Beth flicked through the book, her cup of tea sitting untouched beside her. It was amazing how many different sorts of bird there were. She could identify blackbirds and robins but that was it. She squinted through the window glass at the new bird feeder in the back garden. She'd managed a trip to the nearest big town a half hour's drive away, and bought the feeder plus three bags of assorted seeds. Who knew that the various species had their food preferences? She hadn't. She was quite absorbed, to the extent she'd splashed out on a bird identification book too.

'There you are,' she said triumphantly, her finger finding the right picture of a streaky green, black and yellow bird. 'You're a siskin. Never heard of you but here you are on the page, and you're cute anyway, you and all your friends.'

There were five siskins perched on the

feeder now, spilling the niger seed. The *expensive* niger seed. Oh well, she'd just have to drive into town next week and buy more. There was an odd sensation in her chest and it took her a long moment to identify it. Happiness. Plain old happiness. It had eluded her for months. Beth laughed out loud and the sound, in the quiet kitchen, was almost startling. It was absurd that a thing as simple as a bird feeder could bring such pleasure.

She had slept right through the night too. The first full night's sleep since Lisa died. No running heartbeat, those scary palpitations which had at first made her think she was having a heart attack. Panic attack, Dr O'Neill, had corrected. As a nurse she should have known that. But her mind was too messed up at that point to sort it all through.

It was a week since Sarah-Jayne's party and her days had been quiet, spent pulling up weeds in the garden, reading and watching her birds. Her mother had phoned once and chided Beth for not searching for work. But Beth refused to feel guilty or lazy, both of which were heavily implied by Milly Hainshaw, if not quite said out loud. Her mother was, for once, restrained enough not to go for the jugular.

The truth was that Beth wasn't restless yet. Once she got restless, then she'd look for agency work. She had found the nearest hospital, which was an hour's drive away, but there was a cottage hospital too, a little closer, which might offer some hours. That was it. Vague and incomplete plans. She'd get there. Just not yet.

She wondered how Sarah-Jayne was doing, and if the party had ended soon after she left or kept going into the small hours. Which took her right on to thinking about Alex. They hadn't quarrelled but they hadn't parted the best of friends either. He'd been brusque with her when she'd thought he was going to go for Darren White. How was she to know he wasn't the kind of man to let fly with his fists? *She could've given him the benefit of the doubt.* Well, that was two apologies she owed him, then — she hadn't said sorry yet for her coolness the day they met. Was she going to get a chance to make those apologies? She hadn't seen him since the party. She mulled it over, drinking her now cold tea. It stood to reason. He'd said business was busy and he had no excuse to visit her. Besides, if she really wanted to see him she could pop next door. *I don't want to see him. I'm happy here by myself.*

It was foolish to encourage a friendship with him. They had so little in common. Beth gripped the cup handle as she remembered him talking about his fiancée, Gillian. It was tragic, a young life cut short. But she didn't get it. Didn't understand why it had driven Alex to take further risks with his own life. And she was reminded of his warning. He had no dependents and no intention of gathering any. He couldn't have made it any clearer if he'd taken out an advert on social media. So, he too, didn't want to encourage any closer bond between them. That was fine by her.

She put her cup down and glanced out

at the feeder to see if any new visitors had arrived, but the birds had all flown, leaving a scattering of seed and a single green feather. On the fence sat an enormously fat tabby cat. Beth jumped up and knocked hard on the glass.

'Shoo! Scat, cat. Oh!' she said in frustration, as the beast blinked its yellow eyes at her but didn't budge an inch.

The doorbell rang. Muttering a promise to the cat that she'd be back, Beth went to get the door. Alex stood on her doorstep.

'Can I come in?' He didn't wait for her invitation but stepped forward.

Beth had no choice but to back into the tiny hallway and then lead the way to the kitchen. It was a brighter, more cheerful room than the living room and was where she spent most of her time.

'Tea?' she offered.

'No, thanks. I see Tony's made your acquaintance.' Alex nodded over her head to the window.

'Who's Tony?' Beth turned, wondering if there was someone in her garden. No, just the huge cat. '*That's* Tony? Please don't tell me he's yours. He's just scared off all my lovely birds.'

'You don't need to worry. Tony's bird-catching days are behind him. The birds will soon be back, I promise. He kind of defies the laws of gravity, sitting on that fence, doesn't he?'

Beth looked out to where the cat was perched on the narrow width of the wooden fence like a particularly fine circus performer. A laugh gurgled up spontaneously from her throat and Alex was laughing too. It felt good to share the humour.

'About the party ...'

'Last week, I ...'

They both spoke at once.

Beth smiled. 'You first.'

'I wanted to apologise. I was rather abrupt with you. I don't often share what happened to Gillian and, well, I was probably too brutally honest with the telling of it.'

'I'm sorry too,' Beth said, and it was as if Alex's apology had loosened something in her chest and allowed her to speak truthfully. 'I should've realised you wouldn't attack Darren White. It was stupid of me to cry out.'

Alex shook his head. 'You didn't know how I'd react. We don't know each other well enough to predict what the other's behaviour will be. So you don't need to apologise to me, Beth.'

'If not for that, then I do need to say sorry for the way we met. I wasn't very welcoming, especially since you were there to fix the tap and do me a favour. I can only put it down to the fact that I haven't been very well lately.'

'You do seem determined to apologise one way or another,' Alex grinned, 'so I'll accept it if we can start afresh?'

'Yes, I'd like that.' A warm glow enveloped her at his words. Could they be friends after all, despite their differences? Beth hoped so.

'You said you haven't been well; can I ask what it was? You don't need to tell me of course, if you don't wish to. I don't want to pry.'

'It's no secret, even if my mother would

rather it was.' Beth sank back onto one of the blue-cushioned kitchen stools and Alex took the other. 'As I told you, I was a nurse. I worked in a hospice in London, for cancer patients. I worked there for ten years and enjoyed it, despite its sad moments, because I felt I was making a difference, you know? Even though there could be no happy endings for any of my patients, I could ease their last weeks, make sure they were comfortable and, for some at least, at peace.'

'It sounds like a hard job.'

'Yes, but I could handle it. Or thought I could. I wonder now if the burn out I was warned about was a slow one, that it began the day I started there and that I would always have reached the tipping point by the end of a decade. Who knows? All I know is that when I met Lisa, I met someone very special. She was sixteen when she arrived at the hospice, and over the months we became very close. She was like a younger sister to me. In a funny way, she was the strong one. Because as she became physically weaker and we knew the end was in sight, she would grip my hand. It looked as if she needed comfort when she did that, but we both knew she was giving me strength to go on. Lisa had made her peace with the world. But I hadn't. I wasn't ready to let her go. Of course, it didn't matter how skilled a nurse I was or how much energy I channelled into her care. In the end, she slipped away.'

Beth's throat caught. She was barely aware of Alex reaching out and grasping her cold fingers in his large, warm hand.

'You did all you could,' he said.

Beth nodded. 'I did all I could, but it wasn't enough. That was when I broke down. I was so angry — it felt like I had failed her. Logically, I know there was no other possible outcome, but at the time, I lost sight of that. I still feel it when I think about her, the sense of frustration and helplessness. How could I function as a nurse, feeling like that? The short answer is that I couldn't. I can't. I was given time off. Or rather, I was ordered to the doctor by my boss. My doctor advised me to take a complete rest. It says 'stress' on the doctor's line. My mother didn't like that. She thinks I'm skiving.' She gave a small, bitter laugh.

'Do you still blame yourself?' Alex asked.

'Yes. No. I don't know.' Beth sighed. 'Some days I do, but I'm getting better. There are more days now when I wake up and the world is bright and hopeful again. Being here, in Moira's cottage, is good for me. I know that.'

She became aware that she was clutching at Alex's hand and awkwardly let it go. Much safer to fold her arms and hug her body.

'I could tell you that you are not to blame and that you need to forgive yourself,' Alex said, 'but I'm guessing you know all this already. Or at least, your head does. Your body is just taking longer to adjust.'

'That's it exactly,' Beth agreed. It was a relief not to have to explain it further to him. That he *got* it. Got her.

'Is this why you are so against taking risks?'

'I just don't understand why you would risk your life. It's hard enough to stay healthy and alive without going looking for trouble. To me, it's wrong and selfish. We should make the most of every day we get.'

'Can't we make the most of it by living life to the full?' Alex countered.

'By doing dangerous sports where you could die? I don't get it. Where's the pleasure in that?'

'Where's the pleasure in sitting at home doing nothing, letting the minutes of your life tick away in boredom?'

'What's wrong with a peaceful, contented life? There's plenty of fulfilment to be had in doing this.' Beth indicated her kitchen, the bird feeder outside, the streaming sunshine whose rays were warming them.

'This is enough to make you happy?' Alex's tone was disbelieving.

'Yes, it is. Doesn't it make you at all contented?' Beth waited for his answer, curious. What made Alex tick?

'Contented, yes. But I'm not looking

for contented,' he said. 'I want a lot more from life before I go. Have you ever seen the view from a mountain summit? Or felt the freshness of the air as you parachute from an aeroplane? Once you've experienced those thrills, you end up wanting more.'

Beth shuddered. 'Not me. I'm quite happy here, thank you very much.'

'Then I'd better not ask you what I came over to ask.'

'What was that?'

'You wouldn't be interested.'

'Now you're teasing me. Go on, spit it out.'

'At Sarah-Jayne's party, I asked you if you'd join the Rescue Team. We could do with a nurse.'

Beth opened her mouth to reply but Alex held up a hand and hurried on.

'Before you say an outright no, hear me out, please.'

'Okay. But I'm pretty sure I know what my answer is.'

'You wouldn't have to climb any mountains or take part in any actual rescues.

What we are in dire need of is first aid medical training. Some of our members are reluctant to learn the necessary skills, but I'm absolutely convinced they're vital. So we need someone with a nursing background to teach bandaging, CPR and whatever else you can.'

Beth frowned. It didn't sound as if there would be any danger. What could go wrong if she was simply teaching a class? A part of her was interested. The same part of her that had gone to the trouble of identifying the nearest hospital where she might find work. The other part of her was screaming 'no!' That side wanted to hide in Moira's cottage and never come out. She'd been tested too much in the last year.

'You could make a huge difference to how well our rescues finish,' Alex was saying. 'Will you at least think about it?'

'Why me?' she said.

'What do you mean?'

'Well, there must be lots of other nurses you could approach. There are two hospitals within an hour's radius of here. Why not go to one of them for volunteers?'

'I don't know any nurses to ask,' Alex shrugged. 'Besides, you're not working, which means you're available twenty-four, seven — unlike nurses who, I believe, have shifts they can't just up and leave. You'd be able to teach a class one evening a week to suit.'

So it wasn't particularly Beth Hainshaw that Alex was inviting onto his team. It was her availability. Beth felt a tug of disappointment. Don't be daft, she chided herself silently, he's right. It's about being practical.

'Well?' Alex said, one brow slanted in concern at her silence.

'I don't know,' she said honestly. 'I don't know if I can handle it.'

'I'm sorry, I'm an idiot.' Alex slammed the heel of his hand onto his forehead. 'You've just explained that you're off work with stress and then I lumber in with my size twelves and ask you to come work with us on mountain emergencies which can also be stressful. What a dolt.'

'I'm flattered you asked,' Beth smiled.

'I am.'

Alex got up. 'I've kept you long enough. I'd best be off.'

'Are you taking a tour today?'

'No, I've got a ton of paperwork for this evening, but two of my employees are taking the tours for the next couple of days. I'm going to the Post to meet Bryn.'

'Can I come along?'

Alex looked as surprised as Beth felt when the words spontaneously formed. She hadn't thought it through at all. What was she thinking? He wouldn't want her interfering with whatever he and Bryn had planned. But then she realised he also looked pleased.

'Of course. I'd love to show you the Post.'

★   ★   ★

It was picturesque, Beth thought, as Alex brought the car to a halt in the car park outside the Post. The old stone house was back-dropped by the grey shapes of the mountains, and the ground around it was purple heather and the bobbing white fluffy flower heads of cotton grasses.

'It's busy,' she remarked as they made their way past ten or so cars.

'There's a first aid course on today,' Alex said. 'The Post is used by various community groups as well as by the team. And before you ask, we definitely do need our own medical training dedicated to the team. If I asked the guys to join this course going on today, I can guarantee half of them wouldn't bother.'

He led the way inside. Beth saw the first-aiders bandaging each other while their teacher called out instructions. There was a lot of chattering and good-natured laughing as they tried to follow what the young man was telling them to do. I could do that, she thought impulsively. It wasn't such a bad suggestion Alex was making.

'Hey, Alex. Beth.' Bryn waved from the doorway of the small offices.

'I hope you don't mind me joining you,' Beth said. 'I was curious to see this place.'

'Not at all. You're very welcome,' Bryn

said, smiling.

'How are the vehicles?' Alex asked. 'Any more damage?'

'I haven't checked them. Let's do that now.'

Beth followed the two men to the cement-floored garage area with its huge double doors. It was draughty here and she shivered.

'What damage?' she asked.

Bryn threw a questioning glance at Alex, who gave a slight nod, before he answered.

'Someone vandalised the team Land Rovers a few days ago.'

'How awful. Who would want to do that?'

'Could be kids,' Alex said.

'Except ...' Bryn stopped mid-sentence.

'Except what?' Beth prompted.

'Alex?' Bryn said helplessly. 'Do you want to tell her?'

'Yes, tell me,' Beth said. 'Stop being so mysterious, please.' She stared at Alex.

'Someone may have cut one of the climbing ropes.'

'May have? Don't you know for sure? Was it … were you …?' An icy shock went through her as she realised the implications of what he was saying. 'You were *on* the rope that was cut, weren't you? You could've been killed.' She stared at him in horror.

'But I wasn't,' he said firmly. 'The rope was partly cut, but it might have been wear and tear. I don't know.'

Beth didn't believe him. He was trying to make her feel better.

'Don't you check your equipment?' she persisted. 'Wouldn't you have noticed a cut in the rope?'

'Stupidly, I didn't check it before I climbed that day. I'd checked it the day before and it was fine.'

'Rather unlikely that wear and tear would set in over one day, isn't it?'

Alex nodded reluctantly.

'Who'd do something so malicious?' Beth asked.

'That's why we're here now,' Bryn said. 'To have a discussion about it.'

'There's been no more vandalism this

week, so it could be over. The person — or persons — unknown may have got it out of their systems,' Alex said.

'Yeah,' Bryn nodded slowly. 'But I'd still like to know who the culprit is.'

'Who has access to the ropes and the Land Rovers?' Beth asked.

Alex ran fingers through his thick dark hair, leaving it spiked as if the wind had blown through it. His blue eyes were serious.

'Lots of people. Any member of the Mountain Rescue Team and any community group that uses the Post. That's a long list of possibilities.'

'These are our friends and neighbours,' Bryn said. 'It's hard to imagine who'd do this.'

'Could it be an outsider? Someone new to Invermalloch?' Beth said.

They both grinned at her.

'What? Oh, I see. I've made myself chief suspect.' She rolled her eyes. 'Not very sensible of me.'

'No, it's good talking this through out loud,' Alex said. 'Does anyone hold a grudge against the team?'

'I don't see why,' said Bryn.

'Do you ever turn people away who want to join?' Beth asked.

'If they don't have the right skills we do.'

'That could be a reason for someone to be annoyed.'

Bryn turned to a nearby filing cabinet and slid open the top drawer. 'In here are applications for the last two years.'

'Hand them over,' said Alex.

They flicked through the A4 sheets.

'Conor McBain's brother wanted to join, remember, but he has no winter skills so we told him to go and get experience or training and come back after that.'

'That doesn't sound too harsh,' Beth said. 'Besides, if his goal is to get into the team, and he has the chance to do that after gaining more experience, why would he jeopardise it by potentially getting caught causing criminal damage?'

'Good point.'

Alex's fingers touched her own briefly. It felt like praise but also like friendship.

As if he was saying *we're a team*. Once more, Beth felt the sensation of happiness. If she didn't take care, she might even start to find it a familiar emotion. She hid a smile.

'Here's two that were definitely turned down flat.' Bryn waved the papers. 'Ben Connelly and his brother Dermot.'

'Ben's gone to work in Edinburgh,' Alex said. 'His mother told me when I bumped into her recently. Dermot, she didn't mention. So he's a possible, though I haven't seen him in a while.'

'He's around,' Bryn said. 'He's a farm labourer for MacAuley.'

'What about Darren White?' Beth asked.

Alex raised his brows.

'No, really,' she went on. 'I saw the way he reacted to you at the party. The man dislikes you, it's obvious.'

'Darren does have access to the Post, and to most places around here; he's the maintenance man. He and I do have a history,' Alex said slowly, 'but I don't think he's the villain. That barney at

69

Sarah-Jayne's party was *after* the rope was cut and the vehicles were scratched. Besides, Darren's grudges are against me personally, not against the Mountain Rescue Team. He's got no reason to try to damage the team.'

Bryn sighed and shoved the paperwork back in the cabinet. 'I agree with Alex. Darren's a pain in the neck but I'm going with the list of applicants. There are a few rejected names in there and Dermot Connelly rings a warning bell for me. His temper's on a short fuse, which is one of the reasons we turned him down. Team volunteers need to keep calm and have a large store of patience. What do we do now? Go to these men's homes and challenge them?'

'Obviously not,' Alex frowned. 'There's nothing much we can do except be on guard against suspicious activity around the Post.'

There was a brief silence, cut suddenly by a surge in noise from the hall. It sounded like the first aid class was finishing up.

By the time Alex dropped her off at the cottage, Beth was tired. She prepared a simple pasta and tomato sauce dish and a green salad, and poured a glass of white wine. She took her meal into the living room and switched on Moira's state of the art sound system. South American melodies floated through the air and she settled back on the cushions. Alex was wrong. This was all she needed to be happy.

When she went to bed, her dreams were full of danger. Shadowy figures lurking in dark corners. She woke, too hot under the covers. Padding downstairs for a drink of water, Beth thought of Alex, attached to the mountain by only a thin thread of rope. It took ages for her to fall back to sleep.

★   ★   ★

Next door, Alex had struggled with a tower of paperwork until late evening. He kept thinking about Beth. Today, she'd been different. What was it that had changed, he mused, idling his pen over an invoice. He ran over the conversation at the Post with Beth and Bryn. That was it. She'd lost her air of sadness while they discussed who was responsible for the vandalism. Her face had been eager and involved, her grey eyes sparkling. She was very attractive when she lost the strain from her expression.

Alex yawned. Time to turn in. He had an early start the next day. He was going to investigate a new rock route to see if it was suitable for two customers arriving in August who were expecting a reasonable challenge. But it was Beth his thoughts turned to as he poured out cat biscuits into Tony's food bowl. She was next door, only a few steps away. Was she asleep already? Or was she, like him, a night owl who stayed up far too late?

It wasn't until just before sleep claimed him that he realised he hadn't said his customary goodnight to Gillian's photograph.

5

Alex's bad mood was not improved by discovering his car had a flat tyre. He'd overslept and hadn't heard his alarm, which was set for four-thirty a.m. Instead, he'd woken at seven, groggy and disorientated, and was almost immediately doused with an overwhelming sense of guilt. Guilt that he'd forgotten Gillian last night. That he had momentarily failed in his promise to himself to keep her memory alive. Each and every day. Last night, he'd somehow been distracted from his nightly ritual.

The guilt twisted deeper into his gut. He'd been too busy wondering about Beth Hainshaw to remember Gillian, if he was honest. And that was wrong. Beth had no place in his life. From what she'd told him yesterday, she had her own demons to conquer. He hadn't been wrong about her aura of sadness. She'd been through a terrible period in her life and she still needed to heal from it. But he didn't need to get involved. His promise to himself, after Gillian died, was to honour her memory and never replace her in his heart.

That part of his promise hadn't been hard to keep. There had been no other woman who attracted him or made him imagine falling in love. There had been no temptation. Not until Beth had come to live next door. So it was important that he take a step back now. There was no need to seek her out, to take their fledgling friendship any further. In fact, he would not. Let that be an end to it. He'd be a polite neighbour and that was all. It wasn't as if she liked the same things as him. He was hardly going to find her hill walking or on one of his favourite climbs. And he wasn't much to be found at home, relaxing his days away. No, he'd decided, as he sped downstairs with his rucksack and climbing boots, they weren't going to be bumping into each other much in future if he had anything to do with it.

He came to an abrupt halt at his car. The driver's side tyre was as flat as a pancake. He cursed under his breath and dumped his gear. He was late already thanks to sleeping in. Changing the tyre was going to add to the delay. His chosen climb was three hours' drive north and he'd wanted an early start to allow time for a carefree ascent and a relaxed descent. Now he'd be lucky to scramble up and down and get back before midnight. Alex's nerves tingled with adrenaline. He could aim for a record speed on the route. Go fast and confident. If he was careful, and lucky, he'd achieve it. His bad mood dissipating, he slid open the car boot to get the spare wheel, his mind already on tactics and route-finding and on which hexes he'd need for the likely condition of the rock.

Spare in place, Alex was just putting the flat into the boot when he paused. His thumb raked over the tyre rubber and caught on a circle of rusty metal. He snagged it with his fingernails and pulled. A two-inch nail came out. He bounced it in his palm, thinking. He could've driven over it on the roads, causing a slow puncture. But the alternative was that someone had deliberately driven it into his tyre. The thought made him uncomfortable. If he took that line of argument, then it made it a personal attack on him. Which could mean that the other damage was linked to him, too. *Paranoid, Alex?* Probably a slow puncture and a result of the bad road surfaces, he guessed. He stared at the sharp iron nail a little longer until, out of the corner of his eye, he saw the curtains open in Beth's cottage.

Alex threw the nail into the boot along with the wheel, and slammed the boot shut. He wanted to be gone before Beth saw him and possibly came outside to say hello. *Coward*, he accused himself, driving off fast. What would Gillian say to him if she saw him running away? Alex Taylor, strong, bold adventure-seeker, scared of a woman a foot shorter than him who had done nothing wrong. He eased his foot off the pedal and got the car down to the speed limit. The road was empty except for a couple of sheep. He was looking forward to his day's climbing. All he had to do was blank out any stray musings and concentrate on the excitement of the activity ahead.

★   ★   ★

Was it wrong to feel safest in her cottage? She was only thirty years old but she felt about ninety. She was meant to be out and about, having new experiences, making new friends and enjoying life. Instead, all she wanted was the peace of the four walls around her and no one to disturb her. When would this feeling end? When was she going to get her life back? Her mother found it hard to understand Beth's behaviour. And Beth was beginning to sympathise.

On that glum note, there was a rapping on the back door, which was flung open before she could reach it. Sarah-Jayne rushed in.

'You've got to help me. Say you'll help

me!'

'Calm down and tell me what the problem is,' Beth said.

Sarah-Jayne stalked round the kitchen like a tiger in a cage. She clutched at her arms in agitation and her hair looked wilder than ever.

Her three children were running loops round Beth's garden, screaming and squabbling, setting the birds to flight. She saw Tony leap the fence back to the safety of his own patch.

'I didn't know who else to talk to,' Sarah-Jayne was saying, rubbing at her forehead now. 'I can't tell anyone else in the village, you can imagine the way gossip spreads around here. I don't want everyone knowing my business. And then . . .'

'What about Alex?' Beth interrupted. 'Whatever the matter is, surely Alex will help?'

Sarah-Jayne stared at her as if she'd gone mad.

'Alex? You can't be serious?'

'He is your brother.'

'Exactly. My older brother. If Alex hears what I've gone and done, he'll be furious with me. He's so ... So *principled*.'

'That's usually seen as a good quality,' Beth said, drily.

Sarah-Jayne flung up her arms in exasperation. 'You don't get it, do you? Alex will kill me if he gets wind of this. So you have to help me. You do.'

'If you told me what we're talking about, maybe I could help,' Beth said, and immediately regretted it.

Why would she put her energies into sorting out Sarah-Jayne? Why was it that the Invermalloch inhabitants kept pushing themselves into her life?

'I had to get the stuff from somewhere, didn't I? How else was I going to fulfil the promises I made? Jade! Get off that tree. You'll break a leg. Don't let Skye and Peri out of the garden, okay.'

Once she'd finished shouting at her children, Sarah-Jayne sank down on the chair opposite Beth and put her head in her hands. Beth felt sympathy well up. Whatever was bothering Alex's sister, it was clear she was very upset. But what was she talking about?

'Look, I can't help you until you explain what you've done. Or not done. Take a deep breath and tell me.'

'Okay. I told you Andrew's working abroad and I'm at home looking after the kids. But everything's so expensive, and I get bored in the house all day — so I thought I'd try to start up a bit of a cottage industry, to make some money towards the household. You saw the place, it's practically falling apart and I thought — I *hoped* — I could save up some cash to get repairs done. It was to be a lovely surprise for Andrew when he gets home.' Sarah-Jayne took a deep breath.

'But it didn't turn out that way?' Beth prompted gently.

'I started making jams and preserves, that sort of thing. I'm good at them and I've got my granny's old recipes, which are great. I also made cakes for friends and they went down well, and word spread, so I was making quite a few. But the ingredients aren't cheap and I was needing to bulk buy, so I started to look for a supplier. Which is when Darren said he could get everything for me at a discount.' She sighed.

Beth's heart sank at the mention of Darren. Just what was Sarah-Jayne going to say now?

'The thing is, I'd taken all these orders from people but I didn't have enough money to pay for the ingredients. So Darren said it was alright, he'd get it and I could pay him back later.'

'But he didn't come up with the goods?' Beth guessed.

'No, he did and I made up the orders and everyone's happy and more orders are coming in.'

'So what's the problem?'

'I can't pay him back. I owe him.'

'But people must've paid you for the cakes and jams. So can't you pay some of it back to Darren?'

Sarah-Jayne shook her head, sending her curls shimmying. 'I got the figures a bit wrong. I had to lower the prices; there's only so much someone will pay for a cake, after all. So my profit margin is non-existent and Darren's been charging me interest on what he's calling my loan. Not only that, but Jade needed new school shoes this month and the twins had to have bigger clothes, they're growing so fast. Then we have to eat, pay the electricity and gas, the mortgage. I'm out of pocket by the end of each week and Darren keeps putting up the interest. There's no way I can pay him back.' She groaned.

'Have you told Andrew?' Beth asked, realising she should've thought of him sooner.

'No, and I'm not going to. I need to have it all fixed by the time he comes home. Andrew's worse than Alex for doing things properly. He'd never forgive me for getting into debt. Especially to someone like Darren. Andrew wouldn't understand. Darren's a businessman, he has to get interest on lending money. It's not his fault.'

'You don't blame Darren for any of this?' Beth asked curiously.

'Oh, no. It's me. I screwed up. I don't have a head for business, I can see that now; Darren's quite right.'

'He told you that?'

'Yes he did. He's also given me an extension of a month to find the money to pay him. But I really can't see where I can get the funds from. What with the interest, I owe him nearly a thousand.' There was a note of appeal in her voice.

Beth nipped it in the bud firmly. 'Sorry, I can't lend you any. I don't have that amount to hand. Even if I did, I don't think that's the answer. You'll have to speak to Darren and tell him you can't pay it all. Perhaps he'd accept small amounts spread over a longer timescale?'

'You don't know Darren, do you? He wants his money, pure and simple.'

'Look, I don't want to pry into your personal life, but surely Andrew has a salary that covers your family costs?'

'But it's not enough, that's the problem. Before we had the kids, I was working full time too and we had plenty. We didn't intend to have a big family, or so soon.

We're struggling. Which is why I thought of selling cakes in the first place.'

'We're going round in circles here,' Beth said, feeling tired.

'What am I going to do?' Sarah-Jayne cried.

'What did you imagine I could do to help?' Beth asked.

Sarah-Jayne flushed. 'You dress well; some of your dresses are designer labels. I thought you might pay my loan and then I could owe you instead of Darren.'

'For your information, I know a very nice second hand clothes shop in London where one can buy designer labels at cut price. I like to look good, but I'm not rich. I worked as a nurse and we aren't well paid generally.'

'I'm sorry. It was daft of me. Forget I said anything.' Sarah-Jayne made to leave.

'Wait.' Beth stopped her, touching her hand to Sarah-Jayne's arm. 'Let's think this through. There must be a solution.'

'You'll help?'

Beth found herself nodding. She was drawn into this, whether she liked it or not. She'd have to be a hard person to send Sarah-Jayne away without trying to help her. Beth wasn't hard. That was her problem. Her empathy with others had left her bruised and battered. But she wasn't able to easily turn away. Sometimes it took someone with a little objective distance to really help.

She wracked her brain over Sarah-Jayne's problem but could see no easy way out. Eventually, she couldn't stand watching her guest bite at her cuticles any longer.

'It's no good. There's no way round this. You're going to have to get Alex on board. Tell him everything you told me and see if he can help.'

'No way.'

'It's your only hope. What's the worst that can happen?'

'Living with Alex's disapproval will be fairly awful, for a start. Is there no other way?'

'Would it help if I came with you when you told him? He might not be so angry if there's someone else there.' Although

Beth wouldn't bet on it. Alex seemed the kind of man to show what he felt. Having Beth stand in front of his sister wasn't likely to change that.

'Okay. I think. But when?'

'There's no time like the present. Let's go next door now.' Beth got up, but this time Sarah-Jayne stopped her.

'He's not there. His car's not in the driveway. Anyway, I've had a better idea. It's the summer solstice tomorrow and Alex and I were planning to take the kids to Birchwood Bay to camp and see the sun dip and come up on the shortest night. Why don't you come too? We'll tell him then.'

'Are you sure Alex won't mind me being there? Isn't it a family outing?'

She was aware of a sudden desire to be on that beach with Alex and Sarah-Jayne watching the sun set and rise. She'd pick that over staying in the cottage. Which was strange, given she was avoiding everyone and everything else.

'Oh, he won't mind at all,' Sarah-Jayne said airily, her good mood restored. 'He'll love it if you're there. Take his mind off Gillian. He can get a bit sombre around now, the anniversary of her death is coming up.'

★   ★   ★

Alex felt revitalised. The climb had been a success and he'd had the thrill of a stunning view from the top of the mountain. It was late now but the daylight was bright and strong as if it were only afternoon. He whistled as he bounded down the last slope to his car. There was nothing quite like the great outdoors for clearing the mind of day-to-day worries.

His plan now was simple. Get home, get showered and have a late supper. He was relaxed as he drove back down south to Invermalloch. For the first couple of hours he saw nothing but the grey ribbon of road in front of him and the softening evening light. It was a harsh landscape of moorland and lochan and scarce, stunted rowan and birch trees. He loved it all. He couldn't help it. Beth Hainshaw floated into his mind. He'd firmly kept her out all day while concentrating on his rope and where to place his feet on the narrow rock. Now he wondered what she made of this land. She was used to the city life of London, and the contrast between the bustling metropolis and this empty land could not be greater.

With a jolt he remembered she was only a temporary resident in the village. Moira had lent her End Cottage, not sold it to her. And that was a good thing for his peace of mind, he decided quickly. He flicked a checking glance in his mirror and frowned. There was a red Seat some distance back. Hadn't he seen it earlier, as he set off for home? He could have sworn it had been parked a mile or so down from his own car. He shook his head. There were hundreds of red Seats on the roads. Besides, other people were entitled to go the same route as him. He couldn't help checking on it though, every few minutes, to see if it turned off onto a side route.

The luminescent quality of the light

reminded him that the next day would be the longest one. The summer solstice. When the year turned and the days grew gradually shorter as the seasons changed towards darkness. Alex sighed. How quickly time passed. Each year took him further from Gillian; he almost feared that if he didn't have her photograph, his memory of her face would now be indistinct. He had sworn to stay true to her and every summer solstice he renewed that vow. Tomorrow would be no different, he told himself.

It would be good to have Sarah-Jayne's company at Birchwood Bay. With her and his three lively nieces to entertain, he'd get through the day. Keeping his sadness at bay was a must. If he was on his own he'd have walked through the night, exhausting himself with physical effort — he'd done it before. But Sarah-Jayne had insisted on being with him and there was no way she was going hill walking, as she had made quite plain.

She needed the company more than him, he reckoned. She missed Andrew and was struggling with the kids. She might not say it out loud, but it was clear to Alex. He was glad to help out and planned to take the children onto the beach to make sandcastles and paddle, letting their mother rest for a while.

There was a sudden long blast of a car horn and the Seat shot past him. Alex's heart thudded. What the ...? Had he swerved out over the white middle line of the road? Had he somehow made it difficult for the car to overtake him? He tried to stay calm. He gripped the steering wheel and drove steadily.

A few miles on, around a bend, he passed a red Seat in a lay-by. He shot it a glance as he went by, trying to see the driver. Was it even the same car?

'Cool it, man. Cool it,' he muttered. 'It's just some idiot.'

Still, it had unsettled him. He didn't want to get involved in a game of road rage. He'd seen someone driven off a road before because of it. Anger made some people extremely dangerous. He kept driving. The clock on the dashboard told him he'd only a half hour until he got back to Invermalloch.

He thought of End Cottage and his decision to avoid his neighbour. Beth would surely be asleep anyway by the time he got home. Next time they met, he'd play it cool and she'd get the message. *What message?* It wasn't as if she was interested in him. She had been friendly, that was all. The truth was, he was running from himself, not from Beth.

'Damn it.'

The red car appeared in his mirror again. What was the guy playing at? At first, there was a long gap between the two. But as Alex watched, it closed the distance. The road sign for Invermalloch appeared and Alex indicated to turn into it. He made the turn just as the red car sped past. The driver craned his neck as he went by. Alex recognised him. It was Dermot Connelly.

★ ★ ★

Tony was pleased to see him. Alex fed him before he found a frying pan and a box of eggs. He poured a drink of apple juice and cracked open the eggs into a swirl of butter. He cut two thick slices of bread and pressed them into the toaster. Dusk had fallen reluctantly and cutting through it, he saw light from the cottage next door. Beth was up late too.

There was an urge in him to go next door and invite her over to share his omelette. A desire to have company in these small hours. To share his adventures of the day. Perhaps to mull over the strange incident with Dermot Connelly. Beth's grey eyes would flash with interest and she'd be intrigued by what had happened. She might have some suggestions as to what could have triggered the man's behaviour.

But he wouldn't go over. Because he'd sworn to keep away. If he was lonely, then so be it. Gillian was in a lonelier place.

'Come on, old man,' he said to Tony. 'Let's take this grub into the study. You like eggs, don't you?'

The large cat padded after him. He shared out a slice of the omelette on the desk top, ignoring any hygiene rules. He ate to the noise of loud purring.

'What was Connelly thinking, driving like that?'

Tony didn't answer. It was one of the drawbacks of having a cat as a companion. Alex ended up talking mainly to himself. He stared at the photographs on the study wall. Stared at his favourite shot of Gillian. As ever, her blue eyes crinkled at him. Her blonde hair shone with light. She had the widest grin. The same grin. The picture never changed. Gillian never grew older. Not like Alex, who was getting older every day.

It was an uncomfortable thought but he couldn't budge it. Like Tony, Gillian never gave him an answer. For a moment, like a black hole, the thought swallowed him up. Because if he started to believe that she couldn't hear him then he had finally lost her forever and he was utterly alone.

6

'Are you lonely? I suppose I could fly up and see you. It would be a bit of a bother, I do have my lunch club this week but I *could* cancel ...'

'There's no need to do that, Mum. I appreciate the offer though,' Beth said, balancing the phone in the crook of her neck as she scribbled her shopping list on a piece of paper. 'Anyway, there's no airport nearby. You'd have to get the train or drive.'

'Goodness, I can't drive to you, Beth! How can you even suggest that? It would take forever. A nice quick flight and a couple of days to check on you, that's a better idea.'

Beth sighed inwardly and dropped her list on the table. When her mother had a notion to do something, it was difficult to change her plans. The slight problem of a lack of airport meant nothing. Milly

Hainshaw simply visualised something and made it so. Then she'd be surprised and outraged when she went to book her tickets to find it wasn't there. Beth called it the art of not listening to bad news. Perhaps there was some merit in it at times.

'I'm touched that you want to visit me, really I am. But it's not necessary. I'm fine, honest.'

There was a sniff at the other end of the line. 'How can you be fine? You've given up a perfectly good job to go and live in some wilderness that no one's heard of. Do you know, I asked the girls at my club if they knew where Invermalloch was, and all I got was raised eyebrows. It's as if it doesn't exist.' Said with a certain air of satisfaction.

'It's a very small village. It's not even on most maps, but it does exist and I'm here and it's rather lovely, actually.' Beth injected enthusiasm into her voice for her mother's benefit. If Milly thought she was lonely or sad, she would descend on Beth's tranquillity and destroy it. The truth was that Beth did like Invermalloch and was beginning to settle in, but she needed more time before she could face her mother and news about her old life in London.

'Yes, well. The question is, how are you? Moira emailed me to ask about you and demands a reply. So what am I to tell her?'

A tiny shaft of pain hit Beth's heart. She should be used to it by now. Her mother's selfishness. She had actually believed that Milly had phoned out of her own concern for her daughter. How ridiculous of her. After all these years, surely she knew her own parent better by now. She was only phoning to check up on Beth so that she could answer Moira's queries.

'You can tell her that I'm happy and that I'm grateful for the use of her cottage.'

'Can I tell her that you're ready to give the cottage back and return to London?'

'I told you, I don't have a job to come back to. I handed in my notice before my doctor's note even ran out. I wouldn't have thought Sister McLaren would want me back.'

'I'm quite sure she would. And if not, there are plenty of opportunities in London for you to find a new job. They're crying out for nurses.'

'I'm not ready.' It came out abruptly and there was an awkward silence for a moment.

'There's no need to take that tone with me. I'm only trying to help you.'

Beth bit her tongue. 'I know, Mum. But I'm not looking for work right now. Moira said I could stay here as long as I needed to.'

'She's only helping you to spite me,' Milly squawked down the phone. 'She knows I disapprove of you running away. Hiding from life is not an answer. You have to face your problems. That's the problem with your generation, no backbone.'

'I've got to go. I'll speak to you next week. Love you.' Beth cut the connection and slammed the phone down hard on the table.

She clenched her fists until it hurt. Then with a cry of frustration she slammed them on the wood. They stung horribly. Try as she might, she couldn't get Milly's words out of her head. *Hiding*. Is that what Beth was doing? *Running away*. Was she a coward, as her mother heavily implied? Should she give up the cottage and return to London?

She slumped onto a chair. She couldn't face going back to the city. Going back to a frantic, stressful job which involved life and death, and the awful remorselessness of the patients' and relatives' grief. If that made her a coward, then she was. She was hiding in Invermalloch. Her mother thought her weak. Is that how everyone saw her? Did Alex think that? Although really, why did it matter what he thought of her? And why was he always in the forefront of her mind?

'Enough!' she told herself. 'I don't care what Alex Taylor thinks of me. I don't even like him. And he clearly doesn't like me, as he's avoiding me like the plague.'

With a shaky hand, she picked up her

shopping list, determined to forget the telephone conversation and to forget her neighbour. She'd concentrate on what was needed for the summer solstice. Yes, Alex would be there, but with Sarah-Jayne's lively company there'd be no need for Beth to chat too much to him. She could entertain the children and avoid Alex entirely.

The memory of the feel of his fingers on hers sneaked, unwanted, into her head. He'd touched her hand as they'd stood with Bryn in the Mountain Rescue Post discussing the vandalism. It had been a brief touch but had left a deep impression. It had made her nerves tingle and her heart flare up in happiness. She didn't dislike Alex. The thought that someone had cut his climbing rope deliberately had terrified her — although she told herself now that she'd feel that fear for anyone. It wasn't because it was Alex. She'd care about any human being at risk.

★　★　★

The camping store in town was a massive, sprawling, concrete building. Beth parked her car and grabbed her bag. If she was going to join Alex and Sarah-Jayne for the solstice at Birchwood Bay then she needed her own tent and all the paraphernalia that went with it. Feeling daunted already, she went through the sliding doors into an alien world. It was a place full of equipment she'd never seen before and thronged by fit-looking people wearing hiking boots and thermal tops who all appeared to know exactly what they needed.

'Can I help you?' A young woman smiled sympathetically at her.

'Yes please,' Beth said with a rush of relief. She found her list and handed it over. 'I need all this stuff.'

'What is it you're going to be doing?' The girl asked, frowning at Beth's list. Beth told her.

She shook her head. 'You don't need half of this. Come along and I'll get you kitted out.'

An hour later, Beth left the shop laden

with a new tent, a camping stove and a variety of other items that she prayed had instructions with them for usage. As she stowed them into the boot of her car, a movement caught her eye. She turned her head and saw Darren White. He was leaving the store and he was carrying something. It was the jerky, almost furtive way he was walking that had caught Beth's attention. She shut the boot, her heart racing. She considered what to do. She wanted to speak to him about Sarah-Jayne. Surely this was her opportunity to do so.

He had turned round the side of the building. Beth hurried after him. When she got to the side wall, he had disappeared. It was a quiet spot here, away from the main car park. She wondered why he would go this way. Where was his car? Or was he on foot? She walked swiftly between the rough, harled wall and the overhanging cotoneaster bushes on the other side. She felt uneasy. There was no one else around. She almost hoped she wouldn't catch him up.

She burst out of the bushes into a small, tarmacked square at the back of the store. It was ringed by dusty hedges of drooping dark green leaves. An overflowing litterbin was in one corner, its contents attracting a swarm of wasps. In the other was a security camera on a tall pole with a high-up ring of sharp wire to prevent someone climbing it. It was a depressing place, but Beth's attention was fixed on the sole car in the space. Darren White was fumbling with a set of keys at the driver's side.

'Hello,' she called out, and felt instantly foolish.

Just what did she think she was going to say to him? She hadn't thought it through at all. It was too late now to back away. Darren White glanced over at her with a puzzled expression in his perfect blue eyes. Then he gave her a long, slow smile.

'Why if it isn't Alex Taylor's little girlfriend,' he sneered. 'I saw you at the party.'

'I'm not ... Oh, never mind.' Beth tried to stand her ground as the man swaggered over to her.

Her throat tightened. He was taller than she remembered. Much taller than her. He smelt of sweat and cheap aftershave.

'What do you want?' Darren said, his gaze roving over her in an unpleasant way.

Beth glanced up at the security camera and hoped it worked. 'I just wanted to talk to you.' Her voice died away.

'Talk to me? How nice. Bored with old Alex already? Need someone younger and better looking?' He grinned, showing perfect white teeth. Movie star looks, as Sarah-Jayne had said. Her skin crept at his nearness and she desperately wanted to take a step back. But she didn't. He was trying to intimidate her and it would not work. But it took all her willpower to stand in front of him as if she was relaxed. As if he didn't scare her.

'I saw you at Sarah-Jayne's party,' he said again. 'You and Alex together. What do you see in him?'

The conversation was being side tracked. Beth didn't want to talk about

Alex with this man. She wanted to talk about Sarah-Jayne. But Darren was speaking again.

'I'm not afraid of him. He wants a fight, I'll give him a fight. Only reason I didn't bust him up that night is because of his sister. She didn't want trouble at her party.'

And that's why you ran away. Beth didn't dare say it out loud. 'Alex didn't want trouble either.'

'You think he got the better of me,' Darren said, as if he had read her mind, 'but ask Alex how he got his nose broken. I can take him any time I choose to.'

Beth was surprised. Had Darren White really broken Alex's nose? It didn't seem likely. If that was the case, why had Darren been scared of Alex the night of the party?

'What do you want? Because I've got work to do.' Darren stepped back from her and made to turn back to his car.

'It's about Sarah-Jayne,' Beth said loudly, her confidence increasing now that he'd made some distance between them. 'About her debt.'

Now he was right back at her. Beth shrank from him. She couldn't help it. His eyes were cold and assessing. He was right inside her personal space. She felt his breath on her face.

'What has Sarah-Jayne been saying to you?'

'That she owes you money. And that she can't pay it back immediately.'

'So she sent you to plead with me about it?'

'No, she didn't. I came of my own accord to ask you to give her more time to find the cash.'

'How sweet,' he mocked. 'You think if you bat your pretty eyelashes at me, I'll just drop the debt, is that it? Or are you offering something more?' He leered and Beth did step back, acutely aware that there was no one else around. The neglected shrubs seemed suddenly thicker and darker; anything that happened here would go unnoticed.

'Tell Sarah-Jayne she'd better get that money to me by the end of the month.'

'Or what?' Beth whispered.

'She doesn't want to find out what. And tell her she'd better not involve that brother of hers. If she does that, I'll double the amount.'

'You can't do that,' Beth protested. The words died away at the look on his face.

She turned and ran down the path, the cotoneaster bushes scratching her face and tugging at her hair. Her back felt exposed, as if any moment he'd reach out and grab her. But when she dared look back, there was no one there. Her chest was pounding and her throat was dry. Beth got her keys, jumped into her car and locked the doors. A long breath slid out of her mouth. She took in a shuddering gulp of air. She felt faintly sick.

She pressed her fingers to her mouth until the feeling passed. She hadn't managed to help Sarah-Jayne at all. In fact, she'd made it worse. Now they couldn't ask Alex for help. Darren White wanted his money and he hadn't agreed to an extension of time. There was an aura of menace about him and Beth knew that

Sarah-Jayne would have to find the cash somehow. His threat was all too real.

She managed to get the car engine started and to focus on driving safely out of the space between the other cars and head towards the exit sign. Except that once there she stopped the car, making the driver behind sound his horn impatiently. The object that Darren had bought in the store had been propped against his car when he came to speak to her. Now she realised what it was. A kind of a pick axe. She'd seen them on the racks in the store next to the winter clothing. Climbers used them for going up ice walls. So what was Darren White doing with one of them?

7

Beth packed her new rucksack for Birchwood Bay. She glanced at the wall clock. Sarah-Jayne had said to meet at the Bay at five p.m. That way there was enough time to find a camping spot, put up the tents and make dinner before relaxing the evening away and watching the stars appear. It sounded idyllic the way she described it and Beth was looking forward to the trip.

She picked up her rucksack and tried it on her back. It was heavy but she could carry it. She took the handle of her lightweight tent and tried it. Yes, it was okay but she was glad Sarah-Jayne had told her that they could park close to the beach. Not too far to lug her tent and gear. She put her stuff at the front door and went round the cottage, making certain the windows were shut and bolted. She didn't want to look too closely at her motives, but Darren White wasn't far from her mind. A faint anxiety lingered uneasily. She tried to brush it away. The man was probably all bluff. Besides, she was going to be with Alex and Sarah-Jayne, she wasn't on her own.

'Stuff and nonsense,' she said out loud. 'For goodness sake, Bethany Hainshaw, where's your courage? Mum's right, I need to find my backbone.'

That sharpened things into perspective. Milly's criticism was more hurtful than anything Darren White could come up with. Strangely, it helped. Beth's shoulders went down. Her muscles relaxed. She smiled and pushed her hair behind her ears. This was going to be fun. She'd make sure it was.

★ ★ ★

Birchwood Bay was beautiful. She parked her car on a stretch of sandy grass at the top of a long slope down to the beach. Getting out, she was hit by a breeze of warm, sweet air. Aromas of summer grass, gorse flowers and seaweed mingled into an indefinable seaside scent. Above her, the gulls cried and wheeled, and far out beyond the creamy sands, the sea was turquoise water and white foam as the waves curled on the rocks.

There was a figure on the beach. It was walking in Beth's direction and soon she saw that it was Alex. He had his arms full of driftwood and as she watched, he set it down above the tide line and looked up at the slope. Her stomach fluttered. He looked in his element. An outdoors man, rugged and hardy. Then she remembered his strange behaviour. The fact that he seemed to be avoiding her. She was suddenly unsure of her reception. Would he be glad to see her? She rather thought not, given his recent actions.

So, what to do? She ought to act casually. She raised her hand to wave, then dropped it. Her hair blew into her eyes, the breeze playful. She tucked it behind her ears once more. She turned back to her car. She'd unpack the tent and rucksack. That was useful activity. And it gave her a few moments to compose herself. Alex could do what he liked.

Although ... Beth hesitated over the open boot. Had Sarah-Jayne actually *told* Alex that Beth was joining them today? She turned back to view the beach. Alex was closer now and she saw his blue gaze and the dark brows knitted above. *Great.* Either he was surprised to see her there or he was displeased to see her. This was beyond awkward. She should never have agreed to come here. Her eagerness for the outing was pathetic. If only she hadn't accepted Sarah-Jayne's invitation. Beth scanned the beach with a frown of her own. Just exactly where *was* Sarah-Jayne?

⋆   ⋆   ⋆

Alex was enjoying the physical exertion of gathering wood. The tree trunks and limbs were smooth from the sea and bleached by the wind and sun. There was beauty in their shape and texture but they were destined for the camp fire. He knew from experience that they'd burn

111

well. If he was to keep a fire burning all evening, then he'd need a lot of wood. He'd built up quite a pile when the noise of a car engine made him look up the slope to the grassy fringe on the low cliff. Had Sarah-Jayne changed her mind? Was Skye feeling better?

He'd arrived early at the shore, intent on having everything ready for the camp before the kids arrived. Then he'd planned to make SJ rest while he took his three nieces down to the sea for a paddle. The call to his mobile had thrown him out of his good mood. Sarah-Jayne was apologetic. Skye was feeling sick and so she wouldn't be joining him for the camp. She was really sorry. The kids were sorry too. But there it was.

Alex was disappointed. He'd hidden it and wished Skye a speedy recovery. Sarah-Jayne was talking rapidly as if she wanted to get off the line fast. He put it down to her concern for Skye. Just as she closed with a wish that he enjoyed the solstice she threw in a casual bit of information. Beth was joining them. Please tell her

Sarah-Jayne was sorry to miss her.

'What do you mean Beth's coming along?' Alex shouted down the phone.

'Why are you shouting at me?'

'*I'm not* ... I'm not shouting, it's the wind. I have to raise my voice.'

'Oh. Okay then. So have a great time and tell me all about it when I see you. Which won't be for a few days at least because I think Skye's probably infectious and it would be awful if you got this bug; it's not nice. Lots of throwing up and feeling miserable ...'

'SJ, what do you mean Beth's coming?' Alex held on to his patience thinly.

'I invited her.'

'Right.'

'Oh come on, Alex, stop being a stick in the mud. I thought it'd be fun for you if Beth came with us. You like her and she likes you. It's not that complicated. Let your hair down and have some fun.'

'This isn't the day for that. You know that it's ...'

'The anniversary of Gillian's death. Of course I know. Which is why it's healthy that Beth joins us. Or rather joins you, since I can't make it,' Sarah-Jayne interrupted him hastily. 'Just go with the flow, Alex.'

'Go with the flow.'

'Yes, exactly. Got to go. Skye needs me.'

Alex stared at his phone. Sarah-Jayne had finished the call.

Now he stared up at the car and the woman who stood on the grass fringe. Not SJ and her three children. A slim figure with black hair that danced in the wind. Beth. The woman he was trying to avoid. Now he was going to have to spend the rest of the evening, all night and the next morning with her. Alex cursed his sister for meddling in his life. A life which he had fully under control. He had no desire to change it. Not on this special day, of all days.

He knew he didn't look welcoming as he strode up the slope. But he couldn't help it. If SJ wasn't here, then Alex wanted to be alone. Alone with his thoughts. And with Gillian. He reached the flat ground. Beth smiled uncertainly.

Her big grey eyes were questioning. He ignored the lick of guilt in his gut. He didn't smile back.

'You don't want me here, do you?' Beth said.

Now he felt the full blast of guilt hit him. He wasn't being fair. It wasn't Beth's fault that he wanted to keep away from her. He didn't fully understand it himself.

'That's plain speaking,' he said.

'Why not. Life's too short for messing about. That's one thing I've learned.'

'Look, it's not you ...'

'Please don't.' Beth put up her palm to stop him. 'I'd rather we were honest with each other. I'm rather embarrassed at being here, if you must know. Sarah-Jayne invited me but I don't see any sign of her.'

'My sister called off,' Alex said, digging his hands in his pockets, knowing his body language was defensive. 'Skye's poorly.'

'I'm sorry to hear that. Look, don't worry about this.' Beth waved her hands in the air, encompassing the Bay and the two of them.

She bent down to her luggage and heaved it back up and into the boot of the car. Alex let her. He bit down on any attempt at chivalry. He wanted her to go, didn't he? He was going to watch her pack up her stuff and drive off. Leaving him alone. *Alone.* Yes, that was exactly what he wanted. So why the hollowness in his chest? He managed to ignore it for as long as it took for Beth to slam the boot shut, slide into her car and start the engine up.

'Wait!' *Had he really said it out loud?*

Beth turned with a tentative glance at him.

Alex rubbed his face. 'Wait, Beth. Can we start over?'

She raised one eyebrow slowly. He didn't blame her. It was up to him to put it right. She was going to wait on it. Make him work for it.

'Join me on the beach. Please.' He ground out the words. Inside, a small battle raged. Half of him wanted the solitude of the solstice. Time alone with Gillian and the space to remake his annual vow.

The other half, which was noisier, had decided it did want company. Beth's company. The woman whose interest in the Rescue Team's problems had lit up the air around her. Maybe he did need another human being around him this night, he justified. And Beth was here.

'So, what are you saying? A walk along the beach and then I go home?'

'Stay and see the solstice with me.' His jaw ached from spitting out words.

'Are you sure? Because I don't want to intrude if you really prefer to be alone.' Beth's tone was serious now and her grey eyes sought his.

Yes. No. I don't know. But he simply nodded. Yes, she should stay. He'd deal with it.

'We'll start by putting up your tent. Give me it and I'll set it up near mine.' He nodded across the sand dunes to where a blue tent was just visible.

She trudged along with him as he carried her belongings over to where he had pitched his camp.

'So Skye's sick?' Beth asked.

'Yes. Although apparently it's infectious, so it'll probably be the lot of them soon enough. Why?'

'I wondered if she was avoiding either me or you.'

'Why would she do that?'

'No reason, forget it.' Beth smiled widely at him and Alex couldn't help it. A spear of warmth hit his chest. Her eyes sparkled when she smiled. It distracted him from her question.

'So,' he said quickly, 'can you build a tent?'

'No. I've never been camping.'

'Never?'

Beth laughed. 'You sound appalled. I suppose you've camped since you were a baby.'

'Not quite; I was three.'

'Wow. Your mother must've been the adventurous sort too. I can't imagine taking a toddler into the wilds.'

'My mother was the wild one, that's true.' Alex's mouth twisted. 'But I survived my first camp despite almost drowning in a nearby pond.'

'So you were a dare-devil even at that tender age,' Beth said.

She was teasing him, he knew, but it touched on the differences between them. He turned it around.

'You've never camped. Why is that?'

Beth shrugged. 'I was brought up in the city by my mother. My father left us when I was a baby. I don't remember spending much leisure time with Mum. She was always working and I was shifted around my aunties, who looked after me.'

'That's sad.'

'Hey,' Beth objected, 'don't go feeling sorry for me. You've never tasted Auntie Leila's home-made scones with blackberry jam, or gone with Auntie Janey to the market to buy clothes. That woman had nerves of steel when it came to bartering money off second hand dresses.'

'Sounds nice,' Alex grinned. 'There's no scones for dinner but there's apple pie.'

'Auntie Leila liked apple pie best of all.'

Beth's cheeks were flushed pink by the wind and her black hair was curling like strands of liquorice. Her neat hairstyle

119

was gone, and Alex liked it better wild. She was wearing what looked like a brand new fleece jacket and slim-fitting khaki trousers. She looked good.

'The tent, then,' he said. 'I'll teach you how to construct it.'

'Okay. Where do we start?' Beth rolled up her sleeves, looking determined.

Alex looked at her. He knew he should run a mile. His instincts the other morning were correct. There was something about Beth Hainshaw. Something that wormed right into his skin. But he could hardly send her packing now. He'd invited her to stay. He was building her tent right this moment. What had SJ said? He had to go with the flow. Perhaps she was right. He had survived life and death moments in his sports. Surely he could handle the presence of one small woman?

'Alex? You alright?'

'Yes, I'm fine. Okay, the tent. So, we put these poles together. That's right. Then we get the canopy and drape it over the frame.'

* * *

The tent was finally up. A bright gaudy orange in contrast to the subdued blue of Alex's tent. Alex fixed up the camping stove and was now simmering up chicken stew. The aroma of it made Beth's stomach growl. The fresh air was making her hungry. And after the chicken stew came apple pie.

'Auntie Leila would approve of this,' Beth said through a mouthful of crumbs. She scraped her plate clean and offered it to Alex for more.

'You've got a healthy appetite,' he remarked as he slide another slice of apple pie onto her plate.

'Translated means: I'm a greedy pig.' But she didn't care. The taste of the tart apples and sugary pastry was intensely good. Somehow it was all caught up with eating outside where everything tasted *better.*

'It's good to see you eating up and getting a glow to your skin. When I first met you at Moira's cottage you were pale and too thin. Not surprising, given what you'd been through with your work. But I'd say you're on the mend. Invermalloch is doing you good.'

'Yes, it is,' Beth said, slightly surprised. 'It really is. I have put on some weight and I've more energy.'

'And you'll need it for your next task,' Alex said lightly. 'Can you light a fire?'

Beth knew he was changing the subject. It seemed like every time they touched on a topic which might bring them closer, Alex pushed her away.

'Can I light a fire? Sure, if you give me a lighter. Otherwise, it's a no.'

'What? Auntie Janey never lit a fire in the backyard? Auntie Leila never cooked her scones over the outside coals?'

'Have you ever been to London, Alex? You might get a shock. People generally have houses with cookers and all mod cons.'

'Fair enough. I tell you what, if you gather up those sticks for the fire, I'll feed you another slice of apple pie.'

'Ah, so you've found out my secret,'

Beth said. 'If you give me sugar, I'll do anything.'

He quirked a brow. There was a crackle to the air as she silently cursed her word choice. It was Beth's turn to divert the conversation.

'Is there a flint or do we rub two sticks together?'

'Only if we want to wait 'til tomorrow to get a blaze,' Alex said. 'I'll show you how it's done.'

Beth let out a breath. He wasn't going to tease her for saying she'd do anything for sugar. She was too aware of him as it was. His eyes appeared even more intensely blue in the outdoors. His dark hair was ruffled and she liked it that way. How would it feel under her fingertips? She liked his confidence too. There was no fear in being outside in the elements when she had Alex with her. If a storm blew up or her tent fell down, she wouldn't be scared. He'd fix it.

Now she waited to see how the fire was lit. It was a large pyramid of sticks and twigs, corralled by large stones Alex had gathered from the beach. He took a box of matches from his pocket and lit a piece of rolled newspaper. The flames caught and licked at the wood. Soon the fire was roaring.

'That was cheating,' Beth protested. 'Cavemen never used matches to light a fire.'

'We've moved on a bit since then. Even here at Birchwood Bay. We might not be as advanced as London, but we have a few tricks up our sleeves.'

There was humour in his blue gaze. Beth responded with a wide smile. She was having fun.

The sun was still shining as the fire crackled and glowed, and the sky was a pale, perfect blue.

'I thought the stars would be up by now,' Beth commented.

'On midsummer's day? That was optimistic.' Alex placed another log on the fire.

'It was Sarah-Jayne. When she described this outing, she said we'd be eating and then spending the evening watching the stars come up, which sounded rather lovely.'

'That's SJ for you,' Alex laughed. 'Very imaginative and not at all bothered by reality. There won't be any stars tonight I'm sorry to tell you as it's not going to get dark enough. The sun barely dips beyond the horizon before it rises back up.'

'That sounds kind of wonderful too.' Beth propped herself onto her elbow, lying on the rug beside the fire. 'I'd like to hear the story you promised me.'

'What story was that?'

'The tale of how you got your broken nose.' Beth held her breath. She was treading on personal ground. Would he back away?

'Oh, that sorry tale,' Alex grunted. 'Not much to tell.'

'You don't have to,' Beth said, poking the fire with a convenient branch, and pretending not to care whether he spoke or not. Inside, she was burning with curiosity.

'Darren White broke it for me.'

'*Really?*' So Darren had been telling the truth when he'd boasted of it to Beth. She couldn't imagine it.

'Yes, really. I was a foolish boy who let his emotions fly out along with his fists. Darren was a bully at school, picking on the weedy kids. There was this one particular boy, Michael, who always had his head in a book, wore glasses, wanted to be a scientist when he grew up. For some reason, Darren took against him and he'd get him on the way home from school every day, threaten to punch him if Michael didn't give Darren his money. This went on for a while and then one day Michael simply had enough. He told Darren no.

'I was walking home and saw it. Darren started beating Michael up, and I saw red. I wasn't thinking straight. I waded right in and punched Darren back. Michael fled and then it was me and Darren beating each other senseless. He got in a lucky swing and broke my nose. After that he ran for it. We both got hauled up in front of the headmaster the next day and

126

suspended.'

'But you were defending Michael, you weren't in the wrong,' Beth said.

Alex shook his head. 'It was wrong of me. There are other ways to deal with a bully like Darren. I could've reported him to the school or stood in front of him and let him beat me instead of Michael. Instead I remember the sheer rage I felt as I pummelled him. It's not something I'm proud of, letting such a negative emotion get the better of me. I learnt then to keep myself under control.'

'Sometimes it's good to let go of your emotions,' Beth argued. 'It can be unhealthy to bottle things up. I'm not saying people should lash out physically, but it is good to talk and scream and beat up your pillow and get it out there.'

Alex shrugged. He made a show of fixing up the fire and Beth knew she'd lost him for the moment. He didn't agree with her. But he wasn't going to talk about it.

8

Alex rolled over in his sleeping bag and opened his eyes. The air was warm and stuffy. The blue tent material above him shone with particles of sunshine. It was morning. Late morning. He scratched the stubble on his chin. Wondered how Beth was doing. Had she slept well under canvas? Her first night ever in a sleeping bag with only a sheet of thin material between her and the world.

They had stayed up until the dawn broke the horizon. It had been worth it for the streaks of peach and lemon, aquamarine and salmon pink that turned the sky into an artist's palette. Beth's expression had been a treat. Wide-eyed, open-mouthed delight. Alex had enjoyed sharing the solstice with her. Normally the treat of midsummer was his alone. This year, for the first time in five years, he'd expected to share it with SJ and the kids. Which had made him uneasy. He admitted it. He'd thought it would be tough. Because usually it was just him and Gillian's spirit.

And that was another thing. He hadn't made his annual vow to Gillian. For that, he needed to be on his own. Last night, there'd been no opportunity. He could do it now. Alex paused. He should do it now. Before Beth woke and he had to get up and go say good morning.

But the words, the feeling, wouldn't come. Instead of the sharp pain of her loss, it was as if there was a hazy filter between him and his memory of her. There was less anguish this year. There was more … sweetness. It was hard to describe. As if the horror and agony of her death had thinned, so that his happier memories could bubble up to the surface. Alex allowed himself a slow smile. It was alright. He thought Gillian wouldn't mind. She'd laugh along too as he reminded himself of some of their climbing escapades. Happy days. Wild, adrenaline-filled days. And love. There was the sweetness.

'But right now, sweetheart, I can't do it. Do you mind? I'll make my vow but ... not now,' he whispered.

There was a rustling from outside and the sound of a tent zip being undone. Beth was awake. Alex got out of his sleeping bag and went to join her.

'Good morning,' Beth said. 'I can't believe how well I slept, like a log. How about you?'

'Likewise. It's the pure air here, makes you sleepy. Do you want a coffee?'

'The magic words,' Beth grinned. 'Can I help?'

'You can fill the kettle from the stream while I get the stove lit. Breakfast?'

'Need you ask? I'm starving. I don't suppose there's apple pie left?'

'For breakfast?' Alex pretended to be shocked. 'No, you ate the last of it. I was thinking more of a bacon roll.'

'Great,' Beth shouted back over her shoulder, swinging the kettle and walking off towards the stream.

This felt right. The thought hit him like a full blow to the midriff. He was happy.

Right here. Right now. No thoughts of the past, or of the future. Simply the intense pleasure of the present moment, with the touch of Birchwood Bay's clear air, the smell of the camping gas, the sound of Beth's singing and the thump of his own heartbeat.

Not knowing what to do with that, Alex concentrated on frying up the bacon. Keeping to the task in hand. Letting his mind settle. Yet aware of Beth, his senses alert in case she fell or got lost. He was fooling himself. He was aware of her anyway. Somehow she'd sneaked under his defences. The question was, what was he going to do about it? Let her stay or build the walls higher?

The bacon looked delicious. Alex fiddled with the stove, getting the flame just right.

'Smells great,' Beth said, putting the kettle down on the grass, where it slopped water.

She sighed and sat cross-legged opposite him. There was a little piece of green moss caught on her pink jacket like a brooch. Another frond was stuck to her hair. She looked like a woodland sprite, at one with nature.

'I hate all the bugs, they have to be the biggest downside of camping.' Beth wrinkled her nose.

Alex couldn't help it. He laughed. 'You've spoiled my image of you. I was just thinking how natural you looked with your mossy hair and clothes, and meanwhile you're giving the evil eye to all the tiny creatures.'

Beth brushed the moss off with a grimace of disgust. 'Yeah, well. I'm probably a little bit out of my comfort zone now.'

'Are you sorry you came?'

'Not at all. It's been a real experience. I wouldn't have missed last night's sky for anything. But the camping — well, I'm not sure if I'll do this on a regular basis.'

He was ridiculously disappointed. Which was stupid. It wasn't as if he was going to be inviting Beth to join him at next year's solstice. She'd be long gone by then. But it showed up once more how different they were.

'On second thoughts, I might camp if the breakfast is always so tasty,' Beth said after taking a bite of her roll. 'There's a lot to be said for fresh air and beautiful scenery while you eat.'

'Would you? If I asked you to camp out with me in the hills?'

She finished her roll before answering. Licked her fingers. Then gave him a smile that made him tingle.

'Yes, Alex, I think I'd give it a go.'

'Not too risky?' he teased.

'It's within my limits. I'd manage.'

They sat with their backs to the tents, watching the surf break on the jagged rocks. The sea was coming in and the shallow bay filled with slower, calmer waters. Alex soaked in the view and sipped his coffee. Black and bitter. Perfect camping coffee. Out of the corner of his eye, he saw Beth smile.

'What?'

'Doesn't this make you feel contented? Because you look like it does.'

'You're referring to our argument about what makes us happy.'

'It wasn't an argument, was it? More of a conversation. I seem to recall you said that you aren't looking for contentment. You want more thrills from life. But look at you now.' Beth looked smug.

'You win. I am content right now. And I'm happy.' He drained the last of the coffee and set his mug down next to hers.

'At last,' Beth said. 'Something we can both agree on.'

* * *

She was amazed to find that Alex could sit still so long. Pleased, too, to find they both loved the view. It wasn't just that, Beth knew. It was the whole atmosphere. The tiny stove with its pot of coffee simmering. The fresh tang of sea air. The glorious aftermath of the stunning solstice colours.

More amazing yet, she could imagine camping again with him. She'd fight the bugs. She'd put up her own tent. Hey, she'd make the breakfast too. It was all within reach. Exhilarating. Just as she was getting carried away with her imagination, Alex spoke.

'Do you fancy a swim?'

'How warm is the water?' Beth asked.

'As warm as it's going to get,' came the reply.

'Oh, I get it.' Beth nodded slowly and stood, hands on hips. 'This is a challenge, isn't it? You've proved you can sit nice and be content with the view. Now you want to show me that thrills are good too.'

Alex whistled. 'Phew, that's a complicated response to an innocent invite. Makes me think you're not up for it.'

'Not up for it,' Beth repeated. 'You think I can't swim, is that it? Of course I can. Let's go.'

She marched over to her tent and then stopped. 'I've no costume.'

'You don't get out of it that easily,' Alex said. 'Shorts and tee will be fine. That's what I'm going to wear.'

'See you down there. Last one to the shore has to be first dunked!' Beth dived into her tent as she shouted.

Then she madly pulled out clothes and

dressed fast. This was crazy and childish but there was no way she was letting Alex win. She almost rolled from her tent and then ran for the water's edge. There were thudding feet behind but she didn't look round. Her breath came in gasps. Her chest burned. Her feet hit the shallows with a splash. Alex ran into the water and kept going.

'Show off,' she called.

'I was last in so I have to get dunked,' he called back. 'Come on in, the water's tropical.'

Beth waded further in and shrieked. The water was piercingly cold. She looked out at Alex. He was up to his waist, and as she watched he went under and came up soaked. She shivered. *A thrill, huh?*

'Not too cold, is it? I forgot you were a city girl.' He dived like a seal and Beth made a face.

'I'll give you city girl,' she muttered.

Forcing one leg after the other and trying not to whimper, she went in. Keep walking. That was the trick. After a few strides, she could hardly feel her legs. The numbness made the water feel almost warm. Up to her waist. The icy liquid sliding right inside her tee to encircle her waist. She gasped. Saw Alex's grinning face. With a scowl she kept on going.

'There's a prize if you can get under,' he called.

'What is it?' she called back, her teeth chattering.

'Got to dunk to find out.'

'Dunk to find out,' Beth echoed, mimicking him.

Okay then. For the prize. She filled her lungs and with a silent scream let herself drop under the water. The shock of it nearly made her spit. Then she lunged up with a cry of success. Alex had swum right next to her. His hair was slick with seawater and his tee had moulded to his body, displaying a muscular frame. Beth swallowed a mouthful of water and coughed.

When she recovered, she swam a small circle to keep warm.

'Where's my prize?'

He leaned in and she saw his eyelashes were also wet. His blue eyes reflected the sea around them. His jaw was stubbled and his teeth flashed white against the tan of his skin. And for a moment — a tantalising second — Beth thought he was going to kiss her. Then he swam, putting a gap between them.

'I lied about the prize.'

'You cheat!' Beth swung her arm and sent a wave splashing onto him. Then spun and swam as quickly as possible.

'I'm a cheat but you're a good sport,' Alex said, catching her up easily. 'Congratulations on surviving the thrill test, Ms Hainshaw.'

'Thank you, Mr Taylor. Now can I get out of here? I'm freezing to death.'

Together they swam back to the beach. Beth grounded on the sand, knelt and pulled up, her whole body shaking with the cold. They ran over the sand and reached the tents. As she vigorously towelled dry, Beth had to admit she had enjoyed the swim, if not the temperature of the water. Who'd have imagined it'd be so cold at midsummer? Alex was right. There was a thrill to challenging yourself.

As long as it wasn't too extreme.

Swimming in the sea wasn't a real challenge for Alex. But he'd set the bar where she'd achieve it. Not too easy, but doable. She dressed in warm, dry clothes. The shivering had stopped and her skin glowed.

Where did this leave her and Alex, Beth wondered. Was he going to keep avoiding her after this? He hadn't wanted her here at first. But they'd had a good time together. She knew she wanted to continue their friendship. It was up to him, she decided. But there was something she had to tell him.

Alex had dressed in a fisherman's jersey and old jeans. The wind had strengthened and the clouds scudded across a greying sky.

'Looks like the weather's changing,' he said. 'We should pack up the tents and go before the rain begins.'

'I hope I haven't been too much of a drag,' Beth said. 'I know you didn't want me here to begin with, but I think we've had fun.'

'It's been great,' Alex said. 'I'm sorry I was a grouch. I've no excuse.'

'I know it was the anniversary of Gillian's passing. You had every reason not to want company.'

'Except that I was getting company, SJ and her three terrors, whether I wanted it or not. So it's been pretty peaceful with you. I was spared making endless sandcastles and flying kites on the beach.'

'I suspect you rather like playing with your nieces. I can't picture you as a grumpy old uncle.'

'No, I'm a complete pushover when it comes to Jade, Skye and Peri, and they know it. They take terrible advantage of it.'

'Sarah-Jayne worries about you. I guess offering to come with you is her way of showing you she cares.'

'She doesn't need to worry about me.' Alex's jaw tightened and he turned to the tent.

Beth opened her mouth and shut it. She'd stepped over the line. The invisible line that Alex Taylor drew around his personal space.

'I've made up my mind. About the Mountain Rescue Team. I'd be glad to join as the Team nurse.'

Now she had his full attention. His expression brightened. They were on neutral territory. Beth wondered what it would take to break through Alex's defences. And wondered why she cared. Her mind flitted back to the strange moment in the sea. What if he had kissed her? What would she have done? *Kissed him right back.*

'Great. I'll let Bryn know. So you'll come on Tuesday evening for the team meet and we'll take it from there.'

She zoned back in, her heartbeat speedy from her imagination.

'Tuesday. Right. I won't forget.'

'You look better for being away a couple of days,' Alex was saying approvingly. 'You've got some real colour in your cheeks.'

If he only knew why. Beth hid a smile and went to dismantle her tent.

It was early afternoon before both cars swung into their respective driveways. Beth was considering asking Alex if he'd like to join her for a casual dinner that evening. Nothing special, she decided. Pasta and a sauce. She didn't want it to look as if she was trying too hard. Beth didn't notice it until she'd retrieved her house key from her rucksack, ready to unlock the front door.

'Alex!' she shouted.

He was beside her immediately. Beth pointed with a shaking finger. Large splashes of red paint were daubed across the white walls of End Cottage.

9

'At least it was water-based paint,' Alex said, washing his hands at the sink.

'It required a lot of scrubbing though,' Beth said, passing him a towel. 'A nuisance at the very least and quite horrible to come home to.'

'It makes no sense,' Alex shook his head. 'Why would anyone target you? What have you done to make our vandal attack your home?'

Beth had an answer to that, but there was no way she could share it with Alex. It had to be Darren White. He hadn't liked her interfering in his business with Sarah-Jayne. This was his spiteful reaction. Beth was certain of it. But she couldn't tell Alex about Sarah-Jayne's problems, not without speaking to his sister first. And Sarah-Jayne was obviously avoiding them. Beth didn't believe that Skye was sick. No, Sarah-Jayne was running scared.

Beth remembered Darren's warning. She was not to involve Alex. But now, with the stain of the red paint lingering on her skin, she desperately wanted to.

'Unless it was a mistake,' Alex went on. 'Maybe the target was my cottage. They're side by side and fairly similar. It would be an easy mistake to splash paint on your side of the fence instead of mine.'

'So you don't think it could be Darren White causing more trouble?' There — she'd brought his name into the conversation without mentioning Sarah-Jayne.

Alex frowned. 'We've ruled him out, remember? He's no reason to have a grudge against the team. And why on earth would he vandalise your cottage? He's the maintenance man here. If we hadn't been so keen to get rid of the paint tonight, it'd have been his job to clear it up tomorrow. Sounds unlikely, knowing Darren, that he'd give himself extra work to do.'

'If not Darren, then who?'

'Dermot Connelly.'

'The farm labourer? You and Bryn were talking about him when we met at the Post. If you've no evidence against Darren, what have you got against Dermot?'

'I had a near run-in with him the other day,' Alex said, and described his drive home from the hills.

'That sounds unpleasant, but it could simply have been a case of road rage. You said Dermot has a short temper. Maybe he thought you'd cut him up? Or maybe we're on the wrong track altogether, and someone else is behind all this.' Beth sank down into the nearest chair.

The incident with the paint had shaken her more than she wanted to admit. It was nasty and it was cowardly. Whoever had done it had spread the damage by splashing the paint in a wide arc and then run off without confrontation. She could imagine Darren doing that. A coward and a bully.

'Are you sure you want to join the team?' Alex asked.

'Yes, of course. I told you so earlier.

Why would I change my mind now?' Beth said, surprised.

'Because that was before someone deliberately vandalised your house. Probably the same someone who's got it in for the team. Did you tell anyone else you were going to join?'

'No. I only made up my mind when we were camping.'

'You should delay joining. Don't come to the training yet.'

'That's daft,' Beth said. 'I'm not going to be put off by a petty act with a can of paint.'

'I don't have to accept you onto the team,' Alex said seriously.

Beth jumped up from the chair. 'You're the one who's been trying to persuade me to join. Then when I do, you say I'm not welcome. Come on, Alex. Don't be silly.'

'*Silly?* Beth,' he blew out a breath and looked as if he'd like to wring her neck. 'You're at risk here. And it's my fault. I don't want to get you in further danger. Don't you see?'

'I see that you're trying to make

my decision for me,' Beth's voice rose ominously and she felt herself shake with anger. 'But I'm not going to let you. I will be coming to the training next Tuesday and nothing is going to put me off. Not some anonymous vandal and not you either.'

'Look at it this way.' He didn't bother to hide his exasperation, and now he was on his feet too, making the kitchen feel tiny as he paced. 'We've got an unknown person, man or woman, we don't know which, going about doing crazy things. Weird stuff that doesn't make sense. First off, he or she cuts my climbing rope, which is potentially fatal. Then they follow up with mindless scratching of the team vehicles, which doesn't harm anybody. Now a tin of paint gets thrown over End Cottage. Again, it's annoying but not threatening. So what's the deal? We'd expect escalation in the violence but it's going in the other direction. It just makes no sense. What are we dealing with, here? Point is, we don't know. And until we do, I think we should be cautious.'

'As you said, the damage is getting less, not worse. Maybe the guy's got it out of his system and it'll all fizzle out,' Beth said. 'I'm not putting my life on hold until he gets caught. We might never find out who's responsible. And if he goes away and there's no more trouble, that's great. I'm not hiding out.'

She had her backbone now. The irony of the situation wasn't lost on her. In the bigger world, yeah, maybe Milly was right — she was hiding out. She wasn't able to go back to London and take on responsibility for other's lives. But she could take responsibility for her own. Here and now. Alex might agree with her mother, but she could show him that she had her own brand of courage. She was scared of Darren but she wasn't going to let him win.

Alex laughed humourlessly.

'What?' Beth snapped.

'It took me long enough to get you to join the team. And when you do, it'll be my fault if you get hurt.'

'I can look after myself,' Beth shouted

to the sound of her front door closing. And wondered if it was true.

★ ★ ★

Alex slammed about in his own house. Tony slunk away with a hiss of disapproval at the noise. Didn't Beth understand? There was someone in Invermalloch nursing a grudge. By associating with him and with the Mountain Rescue Team, she'd become a target too. He slapped strawberry jam onto two slices of toast. It was dinner. He'd taken a single bite when the phone rang. It was Bryn.

'You heard already?'

'Heard about what? You okay?' Bryn asked.

'Someone threw a tin of paint over End Cottage. Beth and I just spent the last hour clearing it up.'

'The same guy, you think? That's bad news. I guess we can't do much until we get an eye witness.'

'What's the likelihood of that?' Alex sighed.

'Is Beth okay?' Bryn sounded concerned.

'She's okay. She's refusing to give up on becoming the team nurse. I tried to get her to hold fire, but she's stubborn.'

The first glimmer of Bryn's usual good humour broke out. 'Man, you got her to agree and now you're telling her you don't want her? No wonder she's mad.'

'Did I say she was mad?' Alex growled.

'Didn't have to.' The chuckling on the line was loud and clear.

'Why were you calling?'

'A few admin details we need to go over.'

Alex talked through the book-keeping with Bryn but his mind wasn't fully engaged. He kept thinking about Beth, and whether he had overreacted. Whether she was still angry with him. Tony stalked back in to the room, his tail twitching. Alex stretched out to stroke him but the cat slid past, just out of reach of fingertips. Even Tony was deserting him.

Alex took his sandwich up to the study. It was cold up there. He waited for its usual calming influence to sink in, but it didn't. He was as twitchy as Tony's tail. The situation with Beth and the odd threats had brought out a protectiveness in him. Alex's gaze flicked to Gillian's photo. It was odd, but they hadn't had that kind of relationship. They hadn't worried about each other, both confident in their physical fitness and good judgement of the mountains and climbing.

In a sense, they hadn't *needed* each other. Alex and Gillian had been engaged for four years and never got beyond that promise. Why had they never organised a wedding, made it official? Neither had pushed it, he supposed, mulling it over. They'd been happy as they were. Their lives were full with work and play. Their mutual love of sport had fulfilled them, kept them together.

Alex wondered what would have happened if they had got married and settled down. Gillian hadn't ever talked about wanting children. Their lives wouldn't have changed much with the addition of wedding rings.

It unsettled him, thinking that now. Five years ago, he'd been in total agreement with their joint outlook on life. Now ... he was getting older. At some point, if life had gone differently, he might've liked to be a father. It was an uncomfortable idea that Gillian might not have agreed with him on that.

Alex was concerned for Beth and they weren't even dating. Dating. The brief, strange moment in the sea came back to him. He had wanted to kiss her. Then he'd held back. The moment had passed. Which was all good and correct. He wasn't going to get in any deeper with Beth. He had loved once. Not everybody got even that chance in life. It was enough.

He had no right to worry about her but he couldn't help it. When he thought about the paint on the walls, he wanted to get the culprit and ... His fists clenched. So much for his self-control. The quality he'd boasted about to Beth and that he prided himself on. When he imagined someone hurting Beth, a red wash of rage surged right up.

★ ★ ★

Beth showered, put on her pyjamas and got into bed. She turned on the reading lamp and picked up her book. Outside, an owl hooted as the night creatures ventured out. The air was smooth silver with streaks of navy. That was as dark as it was going to get for the birds and the mice and the bats.

She was used to the sounds now. Even the deep coughing of the sheep in the night, which was such a human noise that it had unnerved her when she first arrived. The owl was a nightly occurrence that she could almost set her clock by. She knew where he roosted — over in the tall trees beyond her garden.

Her anger with Alex had subsided. Sarah-Jayne had called him principled. Beth couldn't fault him for that. He felt responsible because he'd asked her into the team and now she had been drawn into the circle of whoever was nipping at their heels. Perhaps she'd overreacted too.

It was just that she didn't want to give up the chance to be the team nurse. Not now, when she'd got to grips with the idea and quite liked it. She missed her nursing. Not the trauma and the emotional roller coaster that went with it — but she missed the every-day teamwork in the hospice, and the fact that whatever work she did, it was all to help her patients. She wasn't ready to go back to proper nursing but she felt that helping the team was a way of easing back into her skills. Once she was familiar with the limited nursing she'd be called upon at a rescue, she might see if there was space for her at the local hospital a few hours a week.

She decided she'd call Alex tomorrow. There was no reason for them to fall out. Besides, if she wanted onto the team, she'd need to keep him sweet. And that was the only reason to look forward to seeing him again, she told herself. That tiny skip of her heartbeat was all about the nursing. It was not about Alex.

The telephone rang downstairs. Beth paused. She could let it ring. But her sense of duty wouldn't let her, in case it was an emergency. She got wearily out of bed. If it was her mother, she'd regret this. She padded downstairs in her bare feet.

'Beth? Hello, it's Lainey Winthrop here. How are you?' A frail voice but with a sweet, homely London accent.

It was Lisa's mother. Beth had kept in touch with her after her friend's death. The calls had tailed off recently, and she thought this was healthy. Lainey had needed to mourn, and to talk about her daughter with Beth. There was a healing process to be gone through. Beth was a part of this, she understood that. But it didn't make the calls any easier. Inevitably, partway in, Lainey would start to cry — and then Beth would too.

'I'm fine. It's good to hear from you,' Beth said. 'How are you?'

There was a choking sob along the line. 'I miss her, Beth. I really miss my baby.'

★　★　★

Beth's neck ached with tension when she put down the phone and went back upstairs. Her throat was thick with the tears she'd swallowed. She'd listened and comforted as best she was able. Lainey claimed to be feeling better by the time she said goodbye. Beth felt worse, but didn't say so. It was as if the healing tissue over her heart had been ripped open afresh.

The pain and loss she'd lived with over the last months washed over her with a sickening familiarity. If she needed a reminder not to let her heart become involved in any relationship then this was it. She could be friends with Alex Taylor, but nothing more.

10

'Come right in.' Sarah-Jayne took Beth's hand and pulled her inside the farmhouse. 'The kids are away at a party, so we have freedom.' She pirouetted and her gypsy skirt billowed out in a fan of purple and yellow.

Which fit right in with the rainbow of colours draping every single piece of furniture in the large room. There were squares of material everywhere.

'Like them?' Sarah-Jayne asked. 'It's my new business idea. I've sold quite a few and I've paid Darren some money. The end of the month is less than a week away, but I'm going to make it, I'm sure. I'm going to pay Darren back everything I owe him. What do you think?'

'They're gorgeous,' Beth said. 'What are they?'

'Tablecloths, of course. Look, you can see where I've sewn the seams. How neat is that? Plus I'm making matching napkins and I've got an idea for making napkin rings. It's so creative, it's totally me.'

It totally was, Beth had to admit. The riot of fabrics and colours and the grand schemes.

'You managed to pay Darren?'

'Well, some at least. These are going to sell like hot cakes so it won't be long until I can give him everything I owe. So you don't need to tell Alex about my little problem, okay? Tell me you haven't spoken to him about it, Beth, please.'

'No, I haven't told him. Only because you didn't turn up at the Bay. I do hope the kids are recovered from their sickness,' Beth said pointedly.

'I should apologise for that.' Sarah-Jayne folded a blue tablecloth and wouldn't meet Beth's gaze. 'I just … I just couldn't come to Birchwood, okay. I couldn't bear to see Alex's disappointment in me. He's very clear on what's right and wrong. Not that I've done anything wrong, but he won't see it like that. He'll say I should never have got anything from Darren in the first place without paying up front. He'll tell me I shouldn't have got myself into debt. And I don't need to hear it, you know. I really don't.'

'So I take it you don't need my help any more?'

'I totally do, and you promised. Thing is, to make all that money, I'm going to have to speed up my production. I'm quite slow making the tablecloths right now, 'cos I'm on a learning curve. The napkins are fiddly to sew, they're so much smaller than the tablecloths so they take, I don't know, say double the time. So, yeah, I need help.'

'You want me to help you sew these?' Beth said slowly.

'That's it. You got it. I can teach you how to use the machine. Unless you can sew? Because that would be fantastic and really get us going faster.'

'Is this why you invited me round?'

'Yes. Why?'

'I thought it was so you could say sorry

for abandoning me at the solstice with your brother.'

'Didn't you enjoy it? Two days alone with Alex?' There was a sly glint in Sarah-Jayne's glance.

It was Beth's turn to be flustered. She had enjoyed it. She'd enjoyed it far too much. She'd let the fun and intimacy of the camp at Birchwood lower her defences. The paint on the cottage and the conversation with Lainey Winthrop had rapidly built them back up, though.

'Well?' Sarah-Jayne demanded.

'That's beside the point,' Beth said primly. 'You were meant to be there. You let Alex down.'

Sarah-Jayne made a rude noise. 'He won't care if I was there or not. Give Alex some wilderness and a tent, he's perfectly happy with his own company. He doesn't need anyone else when he's outside.'

Beth's mood dipped, hearing that. If it was true, then Alex had tolerated her, nothing more.

'Can you sew? If you can, then you can sit here and use this machine. I found it in the attic, it's a bit of an antique but amazingly it works. You just have to pump it with your foot, which gets painful after about a minute but hey, it's all good.'

Beth sat in front of a small, white sewing machine, still lost in thought as Sarah-Jayne dropped a large fold of cotton onto her lap. Alex might not have been happy to see her at first, but after that, she could've sworn he had enjoyed it all as much as she had. But it was hard to tell with a man who guarded his emotions as fiercely as Alex Taylor.

'Beth? You have to switch in it on with this little button here. Come on, wake up. I'm giving you an easy order to start with. This one's for Amy. She's not too fussy, so a red and white check pattern will do. The good thing about that is, the pattern will hide any mistakes in sewing the seam. I have no idea why she wants one of these. I can't visualise her and Darren cooking a meal together, I'd pin them for takeaways. I know for a fact she's in the curry house every Friday.'

'Darren has a girlfriend?' Beth said in

surprise.

'They have an on-off sort of relationship. I don't know whether they're back together now or not. They had a big bust up a while ago, just before you came to the village I think.'

'Do you know her well?'

'Yeah, quite well. Why?'

'Could you talk to her? Ask her to speak to Darren on your behalf about the money.'

'Oh no, she won't do that. She won't go against him, I can tell you that. She's kind of scared of him, especially if he's had a drink or two.'

That stifled any thoughts Beth had of trying to speak to Amy about Darren's whereabouts on the day of the solstice.

'Why is she going out with him if she's afraid of him?'

Sarah-Jayne leaned across and switched Beth's sewing machine on. She handed her a cotton reel and Beth got the hint. She attached the thread, glad she remembered how to do it, and picked up the corner of the material.

'I don't think it's that bad; she's probably exaggerating about him. Anyway, arguments can be healthy in a relationship.'

'Do you think so?' Beth concentrated on passing the thread into the eye of the needle. Not easy.

'Oh, sure. I mean, look at Alex and Gillian. They never argued at all.'

'They were in love. Why would they argue?'

'Don't be silly, it's normal to disagree. Andrew and I argue all the time when he's home. But you know what they say about the making up afterwards.' Sarah-Jayne's smile was wicked.

Beth cast her mind back over her own experience of relationships. Which took less than a minute because she had few to think about. She had never been in love. There had been boyfriends but no one serious. Her job had taken up all her time and energy, leaving limited opportunity for anything else. Besides, she realised with a jolt, even before Lisa, she was too emotionally drained to give even a part of herself to somebody.

'I reckon the reason Alex and Gillian didn't argue is that they had parallel lives,' Sarah-Jayne went on. She licked the end of the thread and expertly slotted it into the needle. 'Alex loved her, no doubt, but it was never tested. They never did the dull, everyday stuff together; it was all high adrenaline kicks and fun.'

'You make marriage sound boring,' Beth said lightly. She wasn't sure she wanted to hear about Alex and Gillian. It felt too intimate. It was uncomfortable to listen to, but it was hard to stop Sarah-Jayne when she was in full flow.

'Parts of it are humdrum. All the washing and housework, bringing up the kids and paying the bills,' Sarah-Jayne sighed, then smiled. 'But it has its upsides too. The arguments are a healthy sign that you're both individuals who know what you want. The trick is working out how two people can live together and make it a happy thing. What Alex needs is a new woman in his life. Someone who shakes him up a bit, someone who's got different views and makes him question his goals.'

Beth took an immense interest in a snagged loop of thread. There was no way she was rising to Sarah-Jayne's bait. She wasn't interested in Alex that way. Even if she was, even if she decided to stay in Invermalloch and find work and make a place here, Alex wasn't an option. He was in love with his fiancée. And no one could compete with a girl who was a perfect memory and therefore never made mistakes.

Later, when she arrived home she trod on a slip of paper inside the hall where it had been pushed through the letterbox. *Dinner tonight at mine? A chance for me to go through the team routines for next Tuesday with you. Alex.*

Beth grinned. A truce. She was suddenly hungry. She hoped Alex was a good cook.

* * *

Chicken carbonara and a light side salad with fresh strawberries for dessert. It wasn't a difficult meal to make, so why was he hovering over the cooker like a concerned chef? Alex put down the wooden spoon. He'd invited Beth on impulse. He hadn't spoken to her in days, except for a brief telephone call when she'd asked about the arrangements for the Tuesday medical training. She hadn't mentioned their disagreement and neither had he. The first training evening, she'd shot off fast afterwards, without a word. In a way, he'd been forced into inviting her over if he wanted to speak to her properly.

He walked round the cottage for a third time, moving a cushion and its attached cat from the armchair and lifting a pile of books from the floor. Beth had at least accepted his invitation. She had been avoiding him, he was sure of it. Perhaps now she was thawing. He hoped so. He didn't want to be at loggerheads with her. When the doorbell rang he almost jumped.

'Something smells good,' Beth smiled as she came in.

'One of two dishes I can cook well,' Alex said. 'If you come round for dinner a third time, it's takeaway.'

'I like that too.'

Not that he was going to make a habit of inviting her round. Why had he implied it? *Keep it cool and professional.* He'd asked her here to see how she liked doing the team training. Nothing more.

'These are great pictures,' Beth said, looking with interest at the gallery of photos Alex had arranged on the hallway walls. 'No one could doubt you love the mountains.'

'They do all share a theme, that's true. They're memories of good days out. I didn't want to stick them in a photo album where I'd never see them.'

'This is Gillian?' Beth pointed at a central photo frame.

'That's her.'

'She's very attractive. She must have had nerves of steel to be standing on that sharp peak like that.'

'She wasn't afraid of anything.'

'I wish I could say the same. She looks in her element there.' He thought he caught a wistfulness in Beth's voice. But when he looked at her she smiled at him brightly.

'She had no fear on the hills; looking back, I think she hadn't been emotionally tested by life, not truly. She was very young. We both were,' he said, honestly.

'Alex …'

'The meal will be ready. Let's go through.'

Setting the warmed plates out on the table mats gave him something to do. He had a bad habit of talking to Beth without a filter on his thoughts. He poured two glasses of wine and laid the cutlery. Beth looked impressed.

'How did you feel last Tuesday's training went?' he said, launching straight in. No point in circling the topic.

'I guess some of the team members don't feel the same way you do about the importance of learning first aid,' she said, with a tiny grimace.

'They know they have to. I made it very clear that there are going to be medical training days and that we expect everyone to turn up for them. And learn.'

'A word in James Collins's ear would be good. And with Tom Blackmore and his friend, William Graham, too. I could just about raise my voice over the grumbling. It was like being a school teacher to a particularly rowdy bunch of primary school kids.'

'You don't have to take the training.'

'Not this again, Alex. We already argued about it. I'm staying in the team. I don't care whether some of the guys want me there or not. I'm teaching vital skills that could save lives on the hills.'

'I'm just saying, you could delay the training for a few weeks.'

'And we both know why you're saying that,' she said sharply, her grey eyes angry. 'Let's not talk about the vandal. You're overreacting. There hasn't been another incident in the last week, has there? So, it's irrelevant.'

'Why are you so adamant about training the team?' Alex asked.

'Because I know I can make a difference. I'm not ready to go back into nursing, but I want to help people. The

Mountain Rescue Team saves lives by taking people off the hills but it could be even better if all the guys knew CPR and the recovery position, how to support a broken limb and so on. I can do this. I might not be at my best in other areas of my life but this — this I *can* do.'

'Alright,' Alex said, and meant it. Beth's conviction shone through and he knew it wasn't right of him to force her to give it up. Somehow he'd have to keep her safe. Because he didn't believe that the person with a grudge had given up and gone away. No. Someone out there in Invermalloch was, even now, plotting a new way to get at the team.

11

It was a few days later when Alex received a frantic call from Sarah-Jayne.

'Alex, thank goodness I got you. You've got to help. It's Jade. I must've fallen asleep and she's gone! You have to find her. Please.'

'Hold on, try to calm down a little and explain exactly what's happened. Where are you?'

'I'm at Loch Malloch. I brought the girls for a picnic on the beach; it's such a sunny day. I lay down for a doze after we'd eaten and I *told* her to look after the twins and not to wander off. I told her, Alex.'

'What happened next?' Alex kept his tone calm, despite the tension rising in his muscles. Sarah-Jayne's sob echoed down the phone line.

'I didn't mean to fall asleep. But next thing I knew I was waking up and she wasn't there.'

'Skye and Peri?'

'They're here with me. We've scouted about but I can't see her anywhere. You've got to come right now. What if she's gone to the ravine?'

'Any reason she would?'

'She knows she's not allowed to go there so, yes, that's reason enough for Jade. She's got a mind of her own, as you know. I forbid something, then that's what the little madam goes for.' Now Sarah-Jayne didn't bother holding back on her crying.

Alex realised he wasn't going to get more information out of his frantic sister. In any case, it was clear what had to be done. The Mountain Rescue Team was going to be needed. Loch Malloch was a sheltered sea loch with wide, yellow, sandy bays. He had to assume that Jade hadn't gone swimming. His chest tightened. If she had then the outcome was uncertain. He blocked it from his mind. SJ was right. Jade was a stubborn child with an attraction to the forbidden. The hills rose gently from the lochside in a stretch of heather and scrubby birch to meet the higher mountains fringing the valley. The low slope was intersected by a deep, narrow ravine, its sides draped in slippery ferns and stunted rowan. It was no place for a little girl.

'Hold tight, I'm on my way,' he said and switched call buttons. His next connections were to the police and to the Mountain Rescue Team leader.

He pulled all his gear into his rucksack. Since the incident with the climbing rope, he'd been keeping his ropes and harness at home as a precaution. Just until they caught the suspect. Now he was glad he had done. It meant he saved precious minutes by driving direct to the loch and not via the Post. The buddy system would rouse the team and he'd meet them there. Briefly, he wondered if Bryn would come.

As he packed his kit into his car, Beth came out of her cottage.

'Are you working today?' She indicated the coiled ropes.

'No, there's a rescue call-out. Jade's missing.'

'I'll come with you.' Beth's expression was of genuine concern and Alex took a moment to be grateful for her empathy before common sense intruded.

'That's not necessary.'

'How can it not be necessary? I'm the only one on the team who has medical training. That makes it vital that I come too.'

'It could be dangerous,' Alex said. 'There's a real possibility that she's fallen into a ravine. You don't have climbing experience.' *And you don't like risk.* This was definitely risky. Which was why the Mountain Rescue Team trained weekly in hill skills, tracking and bringing casualties off the high ground.

'We're wasting time,' Beth said. 'I'm coming, so don't bother to argue. Give me ten seconds to get my coat and shoes.'

Alex waited, half annoyed and half impressed with her. He was more impressed when she returned very quickly and he saw that her coat was a good quality rainproof and her shoes were three-season hiking boots.

He spun the car fast out of the driveway and onto the country road.

'Hiking boots?' He quirked a brow.

Beside him, in the passenger seat, Beth blushed. 'I know. An odd choice for the woman who doesn't do sports. I got them the day I bought the tent for the summer solstice. They were an impulse buy. I was carried away by the advertising. They seemed to imply fun and freedom. Stupid of me.'

'Not at all. Hiking is fun and freedom. You won't have much use for them today, though. I want you to stay with the Land Rover.'

'No, I'm not promising that. If Jade is missing, then I'm coming on the search whether you like it or not.'

Alex had never heard a steeliness to Beth's voice before.

'This will be a proper search by the Mountain Rescue Team. It's co-ordinated by the police and there will be searchers in teams covering every inch of the low hills until we find her. You'll only get in the way of the rescue,' he said bluntly.

'I don't believe they'll turn down an extra body to look for her and to shout her name.' Beth tied up her brand new laces with a final snap.

'This from a woman who's risk-averse?'

'This isn't about me,' Beth said quietly. 'This is about Sarah-Jayne and her little daughter. I couldn't bear to face her if I didn't help.'

'Sarah-Jayne loves those kids but she lets them run wild. If she'd kept her eye on them instead of falling asleep ...' Alex shook his head.

'Let's not play the blame game. The part where you said she loves them is enough. That part is all that matters. I want to get Jade back for Sarah-Jayne, so please Alex, let me help.'

'I can't stop you other than locking you in my car. But make no mistake on this. If you endanger the rescue effort by getting in the way, I will pass you over to the police and you can stay in the squad car until we've finished up,' he said harshly.

They arrived at the picnic area at Loch Malloch to see a police car and two officers already there. One policeman was standing outside, leaning on the car roof and talking into his radio. The other was talking to the Mountain Rescue Team leader over at the team Land Rover. There were at least ten men kitted up and adjusting rucksacks and radios, ready to search. Sarah-Jayne sat in the back of the police car with a blanket round her shoulders, her two younger children snuggled into her lap, thumbs in mouths, asleep.

'Alex!' She tried to rise and he indicated she should stay sitting. There was no reason to wake Skye and Peri and risk scaring them with all the activity.

'We'll find her,' he said, putting as much conviction as he could into the words.

'I know you will.' Her voice trembled and her face was stained with tears. 'I'm such a fool. I shouldn't have let them play on the beach and I shouldn't have dozed off, but I was so tired. I was up all last night sewing and I still hadn't got everything done. Jade's usually really good at looking after the other two, I can't imagine why she left them. Oh, you brought Beth, I'm so glad.'

Alex let her chat. If that was what she needed, if it took her mind off the awful possibilities of the afternoon, then it was a good thing. He was sort of glad he'd allowed Beth to come with him now. If anyone could calm SJ down, it was her.

Sure enough, he saw Beth run to his sister and embrace her. As he walked away to find his search group he heard their voices, SJ's rising and Beth's calm and soothing.

Alex found the team ready to go. They had split into two groups, one to search either side of the steep ravine. Each searcher had a radio and they would walk a few metres apart on the slowly rising hillside so that they were visible to the next man while they scanned the vegetation for the missing girl. The edge searcher in each group had the hardest task. They would need to look carefully at every inch of the ravine's slopes as they ascended the hill. It was possible that Jade wasn't in that vicinity and that she had wandered up the hill and through the birch trees. The way the men would spread out across the hill meant that they'd find her in the open woodland if that was the case.

'We'll bring her home safe.' It was Bryn, gear loaded, radio strapped to his belt.

'You made it along. I wasn't sure if you would.'

'I left our assistants in charge. There was one tour group today, I guess they'll manage. This is more important by far.'

Alex nodded. He adjusted his rucksack and turned to join the team, then paused. He looked at his best friend.

'I'm glad you're here.'

The team leader gave the nod and the policeman acknowledged it. The search was beginning. Alex looked for Beth, hoping she had stayed with SJ in the police car. No such luck. As they moved out and up the hill, she appeared at his side.

He started shouting his niece's name

and Beth joined in. Along the line, the other men called too, leaving a gap to listen for an answer, however faint. He found himself tensing at each pause, desperately straining to hear Jade reply. All he heard was birdcall and the thin rush of water from a nearby waterfall in the ravine.

How had he ever believed himself immune from this thicket of emotion for his family? He'd blithely thought he was a lone agent since Gillian died. No dependents. SJ had Andrew and the kids. Except that Andrew was an ocean away, and one of those kids was missing. His niece. His small, lively relative who wore him out wanting rough and tumble games and who wasn't shy of having a tantrum or two to get her own way.

He could hear Beth's soft breathing as she climbed the slope beside him. She'd been good with Sarah-Jayne. Perhaps it was her nursing experience which gave her a good bedside manner. Or it was simply Beth's personality. She was pushing her boundaries today. He glanced at her. Her face was flushed and her hair unruly. He liked her hair like that. Wild, like it had been at the summer solstice. He hadn't made his vow to Gillian in the end. He'd left it. Excused himself that there hadn't been peace to do so. But he knew now he wouldn't make the vow yet. Not until he was certain he was going to keep it.

The purple heather crunched under his boots. The scent of bog myrtle rose up from the crushed leaves as they brushed against it. The sun was high and piercingly warm. The searchers were strung out like beads on a necklace. The afternoon had an unreal quality to it. Alex stepped forward. Each footfall took them further uphill. Closer to finding Jade. He had told Beth not to join the rescue effort but he was glad of her presence. If Jade needed medical attention then Beth was there to provide it. If there was more to his awareness of her, Alex wasn't going to mull on it.

Then it all happened at once. In one of the gaps in the shouting, he heard a faint cry. He and Beth were at the ravine side of the search string. He doubted the others had heard it. He turned to alert the search party and discovered Beth had gone.

★ ★ ★

Her heart was working hard. Each heartbeat shuddered through her body. Beth wasn't used to the exercise, she was out of shape — but it wasn't just that. Her nerves were stretched thin. She'd promised Sarah-Jayne that they would bring Jade home. A promise tied to her by the fierce hug she'd given her friend. Like it or not, Beth's emotions were heavily involved. She gave silent, fervent thanks for Alex's company, walking steadily beside her. Her pace was set by his. She was determined not to fall behind.

Then she heard it. A cry as reedy as a warbler. Coming from over the side of the ravine. Alex stiffened and she realised he'd picked it up too. He strode fast across her path to reach the other searchers who were too far away to hear it. In that instant, Beth's instincts kicked in. She ran to the lip of the ravine. In amongst the greenery she saw the red flash of clothing. Jade lay on a small ledge part the way down. Not far from the surface. Beth didn't think. Impulsively she scrambled down. There were small, stunted tree trunks to hold onto. Her feet slipped and gripped on outcrops of stone. The ledge was further down than she'd guessed.

'I'm coming, Jade. Hold on tight. I'm coming.' Adrenaline surged, giving her confidence to reach the little girl. With a final slide on the fern leaves, she landed on the stone.

'Are you hurt? Did you bump yourself?' She was checking for injuries as she spoke.

'Where's Mummy?' Jade said with a sob.

'She's waiting for you darling, just up there.' Beth couldn't find any broken bones, thankfully. She nodded up to the surface, where all she could see was a fringe of vegetation and the dark shadow of trees. It looked a long way away.

'I want to go home.' More sobbing.

'We're going to go home,' Beth reassured her. 'Very soon, okay?'

'Now. I want to go now.'

Jade wriggled and Beth was frightened. The ledge appeared to be solidly attached to the ravine wall but there wasn't room to move about. She didn't want to look down. The river was tiny below them. It was a long way to fall.

'We need to keep still,' she said, as gently as possible. 'Let's crouch down. Is this where you were sitting?' There wasn't space for two to sit but Beth hoped that if Jade sat she'd stay peaceful until help arrived. Beth stood, one hand clutching Jade's arm securely and the other clamped round a birch trunk. She prayed the tree had good strong roots.

Where was Alex? Her adrenaline had gone and realisation sunk in. She was shivering uncontrollably. She pulled Jade closer and waited for rescue.

'Beth! Are you down there?'

Relief flooded through her, despite the anger in his voice. Alex would get them out of here.

'I'm here and I've got Jade. She isn't hurt but she's distressed. You have to hurry,' she shouted back up into the thick air.

'Stay tight. I'm coming down to you.'

Sweet words. It felt like an age before Alex reached them. He was roped up and he made the descent look easy.

'What on earth were you thinking coming down here? You could've been killed.'

'Not now,' Beth said, trying to keep her jaw from wobbling. 'We have to get Jade out of here.'

'Agreed,' Alex said, tightly.

His body language bristled with repressed anger. Beth knew it was all directed at her. She had been crazy, rushing down here. She had no excuse except that Jade needed her. She hadn't stopped to consider her own safety. In a strange way, she understood Alex better. The high stakes of the moment were almost heady. She felt intensely alive. As if every second was sharply in focus like never before. Each tiny frond of the ferns beside her was vivid. The smell of the earth was warmly ripe. The scent of Jade's skin, sweet with strawberry soap. Alex's, all male sweat and spice, and oil from his equipment. Was this how he felt when he climbed or skydived? Was this what he and Gillian had craved on each adventure?

Then she felt the sureness of his hands on her. They made her skin tingle as if a fire had been lit along her nerve endings.

'I'm going to put a safety harness onto both of you,' he said. 'When the team come down, you're going to climb up the rope. Okay?'

'Yes.' She didn't trust her numb lips to say more.

Instead, she watched as the men came carefully down on their ropes and Jade was lifted to safety. That was all that mattered. Sarah-Jayne's little girl was secure. Beth's legs were weak. She wasn't sure she could climb a rope. Or get her legs to move upwards. How had she got down? Where were the footholds she'd used?

Her breath rose up and stuck in her chest. Her throat was swollen. She couldn't breathe. She was dizzy. She swayed slightly in the harness and Alex caught her and pulled her close. She felt the warmth and strength of his body against hers. The hard planes of his muscles. He was solid comfort. She trusted him one hundred per cent to get her up to the world again.

'You can do this,' Alex said calmly. 'Take a good lungful of air.'

She did as he said. The dizziness receded.

'You're brave and courageous, Beth Hainshaw. You got down here by yourself. And now you're going to get yourself back up there. Do you understand?'

She nodded, his words warming her. The anger had gone, replaced with a calm confidence, which seeped slowly into her. She began to believe him. She wished she could lay her head on his chest for a moment but he was bringing the rope to her.

'Take it easy. One step at a time. I'm

right behind you. Now go.'

The hardest step was the first one. Her leg muscles protested as she raised her foot onto a tussock of grass. The safety harness stretched but held. The rope was rough in her fingers. She pulled up. Her fear lessened. Alex was right behind her. He wasn't going to let her fall. There was no one else she wished to be there with her. Alex was her anchor to the earth.

Then her foot slipped. Beth's stomach lurched.

'I can't do this. I can't.' She trembled and her foot moved on the undergrowth. Panic flared. She saw herself falling, falling all the way to the bottom of the ravine. Now it was impossible to move. Beth was frozen in terror.

'One step,' Alex said firmly. 'You can do this.'

'No, I can't.'

'Take the step.' His voice was hard. Bossy. Inflexible.

Beth raised her foot and pressed it an inch higher. It wasn't much. At this rate they'd never make it to the top. But it was all she had right now.

'That's good,' Alex praised. 'Now take another one.'

Her other foot moved forward. She stopped. Her breathing was ragged. Her blood rushed in her ears like a roaring ocean.

'Alex ...'

'Next step. Do it.'

Another tiny movement as her foot went in the right direction. She had never known anyone with so much patience. She was screaming at herself to move faster but Alex didn't accuse her of not trying.

'That's great,' he said. 'Now, I'm going to move in behind you a little closer and you'll feel my hands on your legs. Is that okay?'

'Yes.' Yes please. She wanted him close. As if by being enveloped by him, she'd make it up the slope so much sooner.

'You still have to do the work,' he said, even as she thought that, 'but now you know, if you fall, you'll fall right back on me. And I won't let you fall any further.

You got that?'

Did she imagine the caress of his lips on her hair? Beth didn't know. It was so overwhelmingly reassuring to feel him behind her. To feel his confidence soaking into her. She took a bigger step and then another. When she looked up, she saw daylight. She was making progress.

'That's it, Beth. You're doing great. We'll make a mountaineer out of you after all.' *He could joke about this*. She wasn't sure whether to be mad with him or to laugh. All she knew was that she was right to trust in him. He was going to get her out of here. Her breathing eased and when the lip of the ravine loomed there was a Rescue Team member there to haul her in.

The rest was a blur. There was a crowd rushing about, radios squawking and boots pounding. The police car's blue lights flashed on and off and Beth wondered why they'd switched them on. An ambulance had arrived and the paramedics joined the milling people. Beth was deathly tired. She wanted to go home. Instead, the ambulance crew wanted to check her over. She saw Sarah-Jayne clinging to Jade so that they looked like one person with too many arms and legs. The twins had woken up and were bawling. Beth shut her eyes.

12

Beth slept for fifteen hours solid. When she woke and peered at her bedside alarm clock it stated ten a.m. She got out of bed stiffly. Every muscle ached. Her right elbow hurt. Ruefully, she twisted her head to try to see it. Yes, there was a livid pink scrape on it. She had purpling bruises on both knees too. Try as she might, she couldn't remember how she'd got them. She hadn't felt them in the middle of the drama at the ravine. Now her body was reminding her that she wasn't in top fitness. She was paying for her actions.

Gingerly, she made her way to the shower. The warm water gradually wakened her fully. Padding downstairs in her nightie, she flipped the kettle switch. Coffee, hot and black was the only cure. While she waited for the water to boil, she looked out into her garden. *Her garden?* Correct that. Moira's garden. Beth was only borrowing it. She had to return to her real life someday soon.

As she sipped her piping hot coffee, Beth wasn't sure what her real life was. The birds were clustered on the bird table despite the light drizzling rain which misted the views. The mountains in the background were purple-black silhouettes. When she opened the top window just a little, a waft of heather nectar and damp Scottish air drifted in. She had come to love this place. It was going to be beyond hard to give it up.

For reasons best left unstudied, that took her thoughts right on to Alex. She had invited Sarah-Jayne and the kids round for afternoon tea. She'd invited Alex too. A last minute, mumbled offer before she'd collapsed from his car into her house after the afternoon was over.

He hadn't spoken much on the drive back from Loch Malloch. That suited Beth. She was too exhausted to chat. Her mind kept flicking through the events of the day like a bad movie in Technicolor. It was hard to gauge Alex's mood. So she hadn't bothered.

She drained her coffee and set the cup down in the sink. She had guests coming. That meant baking and tidying up. She took a last wistful look at her birds. There were lots of them and no sign of Alex's cat to scare them away. That was good. Sadly, they would have to perch on the bird table with no one to admire them. Beth had work to do.

Alex arrived as the scones were cooling on the wire rack. Beth hurried to let him in. He smiled and brushed a finger across her cheek.

'Flour.'

His touch left an echo of sensation on her skin.

'You should see the kitchen; it's like a flour explosion in there,' she said.

'Smells good, whatever you've concocted.'

'Scones, and I've got jam and clotted cream to go with them. I want to celebrate Jade's safe return yesterday, and I thought Sarah-Jayne might appreciate a get-together. It can't be easy for her on her own with the children on the farm.'

His blue gaze was warm as it lit on her.

'What? Another smudge on my face?' Beth asked as he continued to stare.

Alex shook his head. 'No smudges. I can see why you're a nurse; your need to help other people shines through.'

'I'm very fond of your sister and her children.' *And growing fonder of you.*

'When you first arrived in Invermalloch, I got the impression you'd built a wall between you and everyone else.'

'Was it that obvious?' Beth laughed, remembering her desperate need for solitude and feeling slightly horrified that he'd noticed.

'Yeah, even to a poor bod who came to fix a leaking tap.'

'Don't make me blush, please. Anyway, I consider you and Sarah-Jayne to be my friends. I'm letting you inside the wall,' she joked.

'Friends,' Alex nodded. 'That sounds good. So, what about those scones?'

They'd wandered into the kitchen. Alex leaned casually against the worktop, his long legs crossed at the ankles, looking at ease. She was too aware of him as she sidled past to check on the baking. She passed him a mug of coffee. The easy silence was like that of a couple used to each other. She sliced each scone and smothered them in strawberry jam and a generous spoonful of clotted cream. She placed one on a saucer and gave it to Alex. He took it and laid the saucer down on the worktop.

'What possessed you?' he said quietly.

'We still talking scones?' she joked feebly.

'I want to know.' His mug and saucer sat untouched. A thin curl of steam rose from the coffee.

She shook her head and took a deep breath. This was like going back into the ravine. Going back into that dark, vertiginous space where excitement and fear and sick dread mingled with the damp odour of the ferns. It was hard to explain, but one glance at Alex's serious expression showed her he deserved an explanation of sorts.

'I don't know, is the honest answer. When I heard Jade call, I acted without thinking. She needed me and I reacted. It was that simple. I was down the ravine before I realised it.' Beth put down the container of cream and tried to find the right words for what came next. 'When I was there, on that ledge, there was this intense clarity to all my senses. It was as if I was almost enjoying being there. I think I got it then, the reason why you like climbing and extreme sports, that rush it gives.'

'You could've been killed. One false step on the ravine wall. That's all it would've needed, because you're not skilled. You were lucky.'

The edge to his voice made her start.

'Aren't you lucky too?' she retorted.

'What do you mean?'

'I mean that every time you climb or paraglide or test your limits there's a certain amount of luck to surviving, however good your skills and experience.'

'There's less luck needed the more skills you have.'

'It's selfish,' Beth said, 'risking your life when you don't have to.'

'And you weren't selfish yesterday?'

She stared at him in shock. 'Of course not. I went to save Jade.'

'And ended up needing rescuing yourself. Which put me and the rest of the team in more jeopardy. Instead of working out how to rescue one person, we had to secure two.'

'I … I never thought of it like that,' Beth said, haltingly.

'What if you had fallen? How would your family feel?' Alex went on relentlessly.

Her mother would have taken it personally. As if Beth had done it to plague her. Apart from Milly, who would've cared? Her aunts to some degree, she thought. There was no one else. It made her sad and conversely mad at Alex for pointing it out.

'At least I did it for the right reasons,' she snapped. 'Not for my own pleasure. I'd hate to die knowing it was my own fault and that I'd messed up everyone else's life for nothing.'

She stopped short. Inwardly cringed. It sounded like she was criticising Gillian. Looking at Alex's face, he clearly thought so too.

'Sorry,' she whispered. 'I didn't mean …'

The front door clattered open and there was the sound of running feet before Jade, Peri and Skye burst in to the kitchen. Beth didn't dare meet Alex's eyes as she greeted them. The twins made a beeline for their uncle but Jade came shyly to Beth and pushed a piece of paper into her hand.

'What's this?' Beth asked, turning it over.

It was a hand-made card. There was a crayoned picture on the front and a shakily written 'thank you'.

'That's me and you,' Jade pointed to the picture. 'That's us in the jungle.'

'Don't I get a card?' Alex teased. 'I came down on the rope and got you out.'

Jade shook her head in a determined no. 'Beth got me out. You got there late.'

Above her tousled hair, Alex caught

Beth's gaze. His was wryly humorous and she knew she'd been forgiven for her comment. With relief she smiled back at him just as Sarah-Jayne came flying into the room.

'I'm late, I know, don't tell me. I had to get their coats from the car, it's raining cats and dogs out there. Beth, did Jade give you her card? She worked so hard on that all morning. Peri and Skye, let Uncle Alex get some air, that's a choke-hold you've got on him. Mmm, something smells good. I'm starving, I didn't have time for lunch.'

She sat at the table in a flurry of kids' coats, long damp skirt and a spray of rain from her wet curls.

'Here,' Beth put the plate of scones in the centre of the table and put out plates and cutlery, 'help yourselves.'

The children ran to the table and scrambled into chairs. Sarah-Jayne bit into a scone and gave a sigh of pleasure.

'Talking of cats and dogs,' Alex said, with a nod to the ever-increasing sheets of rain hitting the kitchen window, 'have you seen Tony today? He's not been in, which is unlike him.'

Beth frowned. 'No, I haven't. The birds haven't been disturbed. Do you think he's ok?'

'I'm sure he's fine. Probably out chasing trouble.'

'You're far too fond of that cat,' Sarah-Jayne said through a mouthful of scone. 'It's only an animal. You treat him as if he's human. I can give you plenty of cats from the farm; they're a pain. But I suppose they keep the mice down.'

'I had a dog when I was small and I was very attached to him,' Beth said in defence of Alex. 'I was very upset when I had to give him up.'

'Where did he go?' Jade said, wide-eyed and with a smear of jam across her mouth.

'My mum said he was too much bother, so he got re-homed. I suppose she was right; after all she was out of the house a lot working and I was at school or at my aunties'. He was probably lonely during the days. I did miss him when he went.'

'Poor little dog.' Jade cast a hopeful glance at her mother.

Sarah-Jayne shook her head. 'No way, don't even ask. I've enough trouble with you three, let alone a dog. Can you imagine what Daddy would say when he comes home? Mmmm, not happening.'

The three girls pouted sad faces until Alex promised them a game.

'Moira keeps a pack of cards in the front room,' he said to Beth. 'I'll take them in there for while. It's too wet out.'

They herded him out. The kitchen seemed to increase in size immediately. Beth took a vacant chair.

'How are your tablecloths coming along?'

'Not good. Not good at all.'

'What's changed? You said you were going to pay Darren back everything you owe him.'

'Yes, but I had only a few days before his deadline and I didn't make it. I gave him some of it, but he wasn't happy.'

'Did he threaten you?'

'Oh well, you know Darren's bark is

worse than his bite. He was nasty, but it's all hot air. He wouldn't actually hurt me.'

'But you still owe him?'

'Yes, that's what I'm telling you. I owe quite a bit.'

'The tablecloths?' Beth prompted. Getting the story from Sarah-Jayne was like drawing blood from the proverbial stone. She talked, but she wasn't telling. If that made sense. Sarah-Jayne was blowing hot air just as much as she claimed Darren was.

'The tablecloths aren't enough. Or rather, I can't make them fast enough.'

'Can I help?'

'I had to unpick some of what you did on Amy's order, your sewing's not that great. Anyway it's not just being able to sew fast. Not that many people want to buy them. I don't get it.'

Beth ignored the comment about her sewing skills. She hadn't claimed she was good at sewing, but now wasn't the moment to say that, as Sarah-Jayne looked distressed.

'Invermalloch is a small market. What

about advertising in the large towns where there are more potential customers?' she suggested.

'Oh, I'm fed up with the tablecloths now.' Sarah-Jayne tossed her head. 'It was a rubbish idea, I don't know why I started it. I *know* I can come up with a good business plan if I have more time. It's like my imagination is scratching away at the other side of my brain. If I only listen, I'll get it. All great businesses start from a single flashpoint moment, don't they? That's all I need. One good, original thought. How hard can it be?'

The rain drummed hard on the glass. Outside, there were no birds on Beth's bird table. Probably wisely sheltering from the weather in the apple tree. She hoped Tony was safe, for Alex's sake. It touched her that, for all his muscled strength and outdoor machismo, he was attached to his cat. He was a nice guy. She admitted it. A good, kind man that she was most definitely not falling for.

'Let's go and join the kids.' Sarah-Jayne leapt up and pulled Beth up too.

13

One step forward and two steps back, wasn't that how the saying went?

Beth was at the Post preparing her presentation for the next training session. But she hardly saw the mound of bandages waiting to be rolled into neat sausages. The computer screen blinked, her screen images unfinished. She'd planned a digital talk, hoping to get through to the few members who still grumbled about attending class. Most of the men, she was relieved to find, were building their first aid skills with no complaints.

Now, it was difficult to concentrate because of all that was running inside her head. Her mother's latest phone call had thrown her. Beth picked up a length of bandage and wound it. Forcing herself to action. Because she didn't know what to do.

There was the noise of a door opening

and shutting. A minute later, Alex appeared. Beth's heart added an extra beat. She shouldn't be so glad to see him. But she was.

'You okay? You look glum. Is it that mountain of bandages? Want a hand?'

'How did you know I was here?'

'I didn't. I came to check the place over before I go back to work. Want to tell me what's wrong?'

'Is it that obvious?'

'It is to me,' he said softly.

Beth looked at him. He had the nicest blue eyes she'd ever seen. Why had she never thought that before? And the nicest way of being kind. She had the impulse to run straight into his arms. To be wrapped in his warm, solid embrace. To block out the world.

Instead she told him about her call.

'It's my mother. She's lonely and she wants me to come home. Back to London.' She stopped, biting her lower lip.

Alex moved towards her. He took her hand. The whorls of her fingertips met his. She could feel every tiny ridge of them. She didn't move away. Alex squeezed her fingers gently. As if conveying a message he hadn't words for.

'And will you?' he said finally.

Now Beth broke the link between them. She put her hands in her pockets.

'I don't know.'

'What about your life? Is this what you want?'

'My mother never stops to consider what I want,' Beth laughed, without humour.

'You don't have to do this,' Alex said. 'You stopped work because of stress. It's too soon for you to go back.'

'But it's not. I went to the hospital today, the one on the way to the town, and asked if they had any agency hours on offer. I've got the necessary forms to fill out. I'm doing this,' Beth waved her hands at all the bandages, 'I'm enjoying teaching the team. If I'm strong enough to talk nursing and to do some agency work, then I'm strong enough to go back to London.'

'So you've made up your mind? You're leaving Invermalloch?'

'I don't know. I told Mum I had to think about it. I have to leave sometime.'

'Moira never uses End Cottage. You could stay as long as you like.'

'I'm so confused right now, I don't know what's best.'

'Beth …'

Then they both heard it. A crackling sound, which got suddenly louder.

'Alex, look!' Beth pointed to the door.

Grey smoke slid in between the bottom of the shut door and the linoleum floor.

'Fire.' Alex ran, taking off his jacket as he did. He jammed it against the door and the smoke stopped coming in.

Beth heard the crunch of gravel, and a figure ran past the window.

'Get out of here and call the fire brigade. I'm going after him,' Alex shouted.

Beth ran after him to the opposite exit. This door took them right outside the Post. She fumbled for her mobile phone and pressed for emergency services. Alex took off round the side of the Post. After she'd made the call, Beth ran the other way to see the fire. Where were the fire extinguishers kept? Should she go back into the hall and try to get one? In the distance, the sirens sounded. Help was on its way.

There was plenty of thick, grey smoke billowing from the stack of junk piled against the front door of the Post. Stark, orange flames licked out too, getting stronger as Beth watched. With a whoosh, something caught and the fire doubled. She jumped well back. She couldn't risk going back round for an extinguisher. The sirens blasted and a fire engine swung into the Post car park. Alex appeared.

'Lost him. Whoever it was knew the area. He's gone into the heather moor. It's crisscrossed with trails and impossible to cover quickly.'

The fire brigade went into action and there was no opportunity to talk more. Beth watched from a distance as the fire was put out. There'd be questions and investigation but nothing would change the fact that the Post was damaged and that it was deliberate.

Alex joined her. His face was streaked with soot. Thick particles of it floated in the air, like black snowflakes, and when Beth put her fingers to her face they came away dirty.

'There'll be an official report, but the fire was no accident — we know that. Someone's stacked up wood, cloth and cardboard at the door and lit it. That explains the amount of smoke. Looks like there was a small container of petrol too, and it went up secondarily. So we had smoke, then a real fire. And as usual, no evidence of the culprit. No cameras, no witnesses.'

'Aren't we witnesses? We both saw a man run off.'

'We saw a figure. We can't identify him. It could be anyone.'

'You still don't think it was Darren White, do you?' Beth said.

Alex sighed, ran his hands through his hair. 'Right now, I don't have a clue. What's the motive? It's not enough that the guy doesn't like me. I don't much take to him either, but that doesn't mean I'm going to go after him. It makes no sense.'

'What's going to happen to the Post?'

'The insurance will cover the repairs, but right now, the team's homeless. There's no point hanging about here. I suggest we go and leave the fire department to clean up. They won't want us in the middle of it when they're collecting evidence.'

'Do you think he planned to hurt us? Or was it a warning? There was the second door out of the hall. Did he know that we could easily escape that way?'

Alex shook his head. 'All good questions. I don't have the answers. It's pretty plain to anyone that there are two big doors to the hall, so if you light a fire at one end, you can get out at the other end. But what if the second door had been locked, or jammed? That's the niggle. How could he know that door would open for us? The fact that he was prepared to set a fire knowing there were people in here is a lot more worrisome.'

Beth drove home slowly. There was

something troubling her. Something beyond the fire itself. She wiped her face with her sleeve and grimaced at the black mark it created. She needed a shower. There it was. The thing that unsettled her. It was Alex's reaction to the fire. He'd gone into action with fast reflex, running after the figure. Which was good, she admitted. *But*. It was the 'but' which needled. It was almost as if he enjoyed the adventure of it all.

She was being unfair. She knew that. He was distressed at the state of the Post. It was going to be weeks or months before the Mountain Rescue Team could use it again. Yet there was a part of him which had thrived on the action. She had to accept it. It was the kind of man he was. It was as if he needed movement, energy and tasks to function. They were so different. It was lucky she wasn't looking for more than friendship from him. In a friend, she could just about accept his restlessness. In any deeper kind of relationship, she would not.

* * *

Alex went home. He needed a change of clothes and a wash. He stank of smoke, like last night's barbecue. Rancid and acrid. He cursed the lack of CCTV. He'd bring it up at the next committee meeting. Right after the horse bolted. Put up a camera now and no doubt they'd never use it. Invermalloch was a sleepy little place. Or had been, up until recently.

He thought about Beth. He didn't want her to leave. The set-up planned by her mother sounded like a recipe for disaster. How could Beth seriously be considering it? Then again, with all the nastiness around in the village right now, he didn't blame her for thinking of leaving. It might be for the best.

With a disquiet not entirely focussed on the fire, he went inside his cottage. It shouldn't matter to him whether Beth left the village or not. He knew she wasn't here permanently. He wasn't a factor in whether she'd go or stay. As a friend though, hadn't he a duty to help her make the right decision? He decided he'd speak to her about it again.

Tony came in through the cat flap. The big tabby was slow and shaky. He wobbled like a drunk towards Alex. Then he uttered a high-pitched miaow and vomited.

14

'Isn't it time to involve the police?' Beth asked.

She and Alex were standing in his sitting room looking down at the tabby cat curled up in the wicker basket. Tony's fur was dull and his eyes were closed but one ear pricked at the conversation.

'And tell them what exactly?' Alex said. 'That a cat got poisoned, possibly accidentally, and is recovering. The police are involved in much more serious matters, such as the Post burning down. I'm not sure they'd be that bothered about a cat who got sick.'

'The vet told you it was probably anti-freeze that Tony drank.'

'He also said that he believed it could be deliberate but that it'd be difficult to prove.'

'I should've reported the paint sprayed

on my wall,' Beth said. 'It's a bit late now.'

'Again, what good would it do? They'd say it was teenage vandals and who knows, they could be right.'

'You don't really think that, though?' Beth said, becoming exasperated.

'I think that whatever's going on can't go on forever. Either it peters out or something worse is going to happen. Until it does, there's nothing much to go on and nothing that'll excite our local police station.'

'Where is the police station anyway? I haven't noticed it on the main street.'

Alex laughed. 'That's because it isn't there. Invermalloch's too small to have its own station. The nearest is in town. There's very little crime here.'

'Are you sure about that?' Beth reached down and stroked the cat's soft fur.

'Until recently, with full confidence, yes. Lately … not so sure. I wish I knew why all this was happening.'

Beth heard the tiredness in his voice. She guessed he hadn't had much sleep, what with rushing Tony to the vet's and then going to work for the late night wild-life tours followed by working the next day. The cat had only just been brought back from the vet now. It had been touch and go for a while.

'Do you think something worse is going to happen?' she asked.

'Are you going to London?' he countered.

'I don't know. I haven't made up my mind yet.'

She had to soon. Milly's phone calls were insistent. Beth had to come home. Now. She'd had her opportunity to wallow in her 'stress'.

'You should go.' His voice was blunt.

'Just like that?' She snapped her fingers sarcastically.

'With all that's going on here, it might be for the best.'

'Do you want me to go?'

There was a long silence before Alex spoke. 'It isn't what I want that matters.'

But still. Do you want me to go? She wouldn't say it. It stung that he'd try to persuade her to leave. It showed how little she meant to him.

'Maybe you're right. I miss London and all its bustle,' she lied.

'City girl,' he joked, but it fell flat.

It took Beth back to the moments they'd shared at Birchwood Bay. When they'd swum together and she thought he was going to kiss her. Now there was a distance between them as if that had never been. She couldn't read him. It seemed like he couldn't wait for her to go.

But could she leave when there was a lunatic around? What if Alex needed her? She risked a glance at his broad shoulders and muscled arms and smiled. As if. Alex could protect himself. He had no need of Beth.

'The police must be interested in the fire,' she said. 'It was arson, there's no doubt about that.'

'I'm not holding my breath on them finding a suspect. This situation, it's like fighting shadows. Some of it's so petty, it's not frightening it's simply irritating. Like having to wash the paint off End Cottage, or touching up the paintwork on the Land Rovers. But the fire, that's intimidating. What if we hadn't got that door open? That's why you should leave.'

'It's not a good enough reason for me to run away to London.'

Her chest warmed a little. He did care, even if he had a funny way of showing it. Plus, she'd said out loud what her heart had been telling her. She wasn't finished here in Invermalloch. She wasn't going until they caught the perpetrator. Whether Alex liked it or not.

'Sounds to me as if you've made up your mind.'

'Sounds like that to me too.' The corners of her mouth twitched up reflexively. 'You're not getting rid of me so easily.'

'If you stay, you have to promise me you'll take care, be vigilant until we catch this guy.'

'I'll promise, if you do too.'

'You don't need to worry about me,' Alex said. 'I can look after myself.'

But she did worry about him. He was physically strong and fit, no doubt about that. He was a clever man and he'd be on alert. Fair enough. But what if he was taken by surprise? If there was another fire, at his house when he was asleep? If another rope was cut more thoroughly? The danger could come from any direction. Alex wasn't superman. Beth was concerned. Not only about the risks to Alex. She was concerned to find that she cared so much.

*   *   *

'Hey, Alex — are you there?' Sarah-Jayne shouted from somewhere outside.

'My gardener has arrived,' Alex said with a grin.

'Gardener?' Beth said, puzzled, and followed him out to the front door.

Sarah-Jayne, Jade and her sisters were there. Sarah-Jayne waved a trowel at them, smiling. Jade, Peri and Skye had smaller versions clutched in their tiny fists. All three children wore green wellies, and along with the tiny trowels, they had a plastic bucket each.

'Where do you want us to start?'

Sarah-Jayne said.

She wore a pair of faded denim dungarees over a red shirt, bare legs and black wellies. A matching scarlet bandanna kept her curls back from her tanned face.

'What is going on?' Beth asked. Her question encompassed brother and sister.

Sarah-Jayne brandished her trowel. 'I got it, Beth. I got my flashpoint. I'm offering gardening services. Weeding, planting, you name it — if it's in your garden I can do it. The girls are helping too, at least until Jade goes to school. Can you believe the summer holidays are almost over?'

Beth remembered the state of the farm. The uncut, wild grass that grew around the farmhouse, and the dilapidated outhouses. She doubted this was going to last any longer than the cake baking and the sewing. Still, she had to give Sarah-Jayne points for enthusiasm. The woman never gave up.

'Have you gardened before?' she asked.

'Some. How hard can it be? Alex has hired me to keep his garden neat once a week. You could do the same.'

Beth considered that. She quite liked the slightly wild back lawn and the old apple tree just the way they were. Besides, someone had cut it fairly recently.

'Moira must have hired someone already,' she said. 'My back lawn was short when I arrived. It's long now.'

'Probably Darren's supposed to cut it.' Sarah-Jayne's expression darkened. It was so unlike her usual blasé self, that Beth noticed at once. Before she had a chance to remark, Alex was speaking.

'You can cut the grass for me. I'll get the lawnmower out of the shed. Then you can weed the flowerbed at the front. Do the girls know the difference between the flowers and the weeds?'

'Oh, we'll learn as we go along,' Sarah-Jayne said breezily.

Alex winced. Beth gave him a conspiratorial smile.

'Right,' he said manfully, 'let me go and get the key to the shed. Kids, I'm counting on you to do a good job.'

While he was gone, the three children running after him, buckets and trowels forgotten, Beth took advantage of the space to ask Sarah-Jayne what was wrong.

'Has Darren done something?'

'What makes you say that?' Sarah-Jayne hedged.

'Come on, when I mentioned his name your face went all funny.'

'Funny. Thanks a lot.'

Beth stared hard at her, waiting.

Sarah-Jayne dropped her trowel. 'Okay, okay. You freaked me out a bit, mentioning Darren. That's all.'

'What is it? What's wrong?'

Sarah-Jayne fiddled with the buttons on her shirt until Beth wanted to hit her.

'Will you hurry up. Alex will be back in a minute. Whatever you've got to say, it's best said now.'

'Okay,' Sarah-Jayne said again. 'It's just … it's difficult to explain.'

'Do it.' Beth's tone brooked no argument.

'Darren came to the farm last night. There. I said it. Happy now?'

'Don't be silly. Why are you defending him?'

'I'm not.' Sarah-Jayne sank down onto the grass. 'Actually, it was a bit … a bit scary.'

'Did he threaten you?' Beth's anger rose. Not at Sarah-Jayne. At Darren White.

'I told you, Darren's bark's worse than his bite.'

'I don't believe you,' Beth said. 'You have to tell me everything. He intimidated you, didn't he?'

Disconcertingly, Sarah-Jayne suddenly burst out crying. The children appeared round the side of the cottage, singing. They stopped when they saw their mother and ran to her. They all started crying too. Alex, looking extremely perplexed, dropped the lawnmower on the small front garden and looked at Beth.

'It's Darren,' Beth said. 'He went to see Sarah-Jayne.'

'Why?' Alex asked.

'Let's get the kids inside and get them something to eat, then I can explain.'

Jade, Peri and Skye's sobbing subsided once Beth had found a packet of popcorn and shared out cups of juice. Beth and

Alex left them with bowls of the snack and all was peaceful.

Outside, Sarah-Jayne had stopped crying too.

'I was at home. It was late. I'd fed the kids and put them to bed. Andrew phoned and I had a glass of wine afterwards. I was feeling kind of sleepy and relaxed, then the doorbell rang. It was Darren. He wanted the rest of the money. I told him I didn't have it. I'm making up the last of the tablecloth orders as fast as I can, but I still owe him. He turned nasty. Said I'd regret it if I didn't pay up. Then he ...'

She stopped and the tears welled up.

'He what?' Beth asked, not sure she wanted an answer.

'He took my wrist and he squeezed it really hard.'

'Please tell me you can see him for what he is now,' Beth said. 'No more going on about his film star looks. He's not a nice person, Sarah-Jayne. He's a thug.'

Beside her, she felt Alex bristle as Sarah-Jayne told her story. She was afraid of what he might do.

'Pay up?' Alex said tightly. 'What did he mean 'pay up'?'

Sarah-Jayne cast a beseeching gaze at Beth. Beth shook her head. Alex deserved to hear it from his own sister.

Sarah-Jayne spilled it all. The cake-baking. The goods delivered by Darren White. Her debts. The threats. The payback.

'You didn't think to come to me?' Alex said. 'I'm your brother. I'd have helped you.'

'I knew you'd react just like this. You're so angry.' Sarah-Jayne plucked at the grass, breaking the stems into tiny pieces.

'Of course I'm angry. I'm furious. What about Andrew? Does he know you owe money to a gangster?'

'Darren's hardly a …' Sarah-Jayne shut her mouth, and appeared to find the mushed up grass suddenly fascinating.

At least she was no longer defending him, Beth thought. That's progress.

'Andrew?' Alex prompted, not letting his sister off the hook.

She shook her head. No, Andrew didn't

know. And wasn't going to. She flung the grass away. 'You won't tell him, Alex, will you?'

'No need to. I'm going to pay Darren a visit. Tell me what you owe him and I'll write him a cheque.'

At which point, Beth realised she was going to have to confess to what she'd done. Her stomach churned horribly. Alex wasn't going to like it.

'Wait,' she said. 'I should've told you. I talked to Darren a few weeks ago about Sarah-Jayne's debts. I asked him to give her more time to find the money. He refused and he told me quite specifically not to involve you.'

'Did he now.' A pulse beat in Alex's jaw.

'He said he'd double the amount if we did.'

Alex turned back into the house. He came back with his car keys and a jacket. His face was set. Beth grabbed his arm as he went past. It barely stopped him.

'I'm coming with you.' She wasn't accusing Alex of intending to inflict violence on Darren. He was in control of himself, she knew that. But having a witness to whatever conversation they had wouldn't hurt. Even if Alex was mad at her. He didn't answer her but he didn't prevent her getting into the car alongside him, either.

As they drove off, Beth saw Sarah-Jayne go across to the lawnmower. She hadn't offered to come too. Darren had most likely scared her too much. Finally, she was seeing sense. And now there was a chance Alex could sort out the mess before Andrew came home to his family.

★ ★ ★

They didn't speak on the short drive across the village. Beth was too aware of Alex. The hard line of his jaw, the flex of his knuckles on the steering wheel and the aura of anger and, she was sure, disappointment. He was disappointed in her for not sharing.

'I'm sorry. I should've told you,' she said.

'Yes.' One clipped word.

She didn't try again. She deserved it. She'd got way too involved in Sarah-Jayne's problems, to the extent of excluding the one person who could really help. She'd believed Darren White's bullying words.

Darren lived in a row of low, brick buildings on the edge of the village. They might, at some time in the past, have been labourers' homes for the railway. Now, they showed their age. The brick was dark with damp and moss, and few had been painted. Darren lived in the middle of the row. Alex went straight to the scuffed door and rang.

Beth sort of hoped Darren would be out. It wasn't unlikely; after all he had his handyman job. But he opened on the fifth ring. He was dressed in dirty jeans and a greying vest. Even the dingy outfit couldn't hide his stunning good looks. Beth understood Sarah-Jayne's attraction to him. It was a pity his attractiveness didn't extend to his personality.

'What do you want?' he said.

'To give you this.' Alex handed him a

piece of white paper.

Behind him, Beth waited. Darren took it and stuck it quickly in his back pocket. The cheque to cover Alex's sister's debt. Once he had it, Darren's posture changed. The swagger was back.

'Brought your girlfriend to protect you, I see.'

Alex ignored that. 'You've got your money. I don't want to see you sniffing around my sister. You stay away from her and from my family.'

'What family?' Darren sneered. 'Your last girlfriend killed herself. You've got no one. Gillian would've been better off with me.'

From where she stood, Beth saw Alex's shoulders tense. She took a step forward. But Alex didn't react to the other man's jibe. Not outwardly, at least. Her head was reeling. Darren had known Gillian. It was a small village so that wasn't surprising. But he was implying that he'd had a relationship with her. Was that possible?

'If you want to keep the cheque, I suggest you keep your mouth shut.' Alex's voice was coldly polite.

From her position, Beth couldn't see his expression, but she saw Darren's reaction. The man stood back, using his door as a partial barrier.

'We're leaving now. The nearest I want to see you is when you're doing your job at Moira's cottage or at the Post.'

Alex turned fast and Beth had to speed up to keep with him. They were almost in the car when Darren felt brave enough to shout out after them, 'Shame about the Post. Real shame it got burnt down.'

'Alex, don't rise to it.'

With what looked like great effort, Alex got into the car and started the engine. Beth felt her chest begin to loosen. She took a deep, refreshing breath. She hadn't realised how tense she'd been.

She was glad when they drove around the corner and Darren was out of sight.

'Darren knew Gillian?' she asked hesitantly.

'He asked her out. Gillian was sensible enough to say no. It was before she and I were a couple. She was spooked by him.

He didn't give up, kept following her around. Until I warned him off.'

'You do see that gives him motive.'

'It was a long time ago. Just another annoyance in the catalogue of history between us. It has nothing to do with what's going on now.'

Beth wasn't convinced. Wasn't it possible that the small incidents had rankled with Darren over the years until he'd flipped? She was going to continue the conversation until she realised she'd lost Alex. The defences were back up. No way to break through. Of course. Anything to do with Gillian was out of bounds. There was a burning sensation right in the middle of her chest. She focused on it, and tried to isolate her emotion. Yes, she had it. And had to ask herself a bitter question. Was it right to be jealous of a dead girl?

15

'I thought I'd let you know that Tuesday training sessions are cancelled until we find another place to hold them.'

'Still no luck?' Beth knew Alex had been trying to secure a location for the team to meet. The village hall was the only building big enough but it was a bingo night on Tuesdays.

'Can't you just change the night of the week?'

'I wish it was that simple, but everyone's got other commitments. It's a nightmare trying to co-ordinate it. Basically, Tuesday is the only night we all have free because we've always met on a Tuesday.'

'That makes sense. It's weird — I miss taking the first aid class. I was beginning to make progress.'

'You were good at it. You might consider teaching as an alternative career if you don't want to return to nursing,' Alex said.

'That's not a bad idea. Especially when my mother is badgering me into deciding on my future.' Beth sighed. She led the way inside.

'What have you decided?'

'Nothing's changed. I'm still staying here for the foreseeable future. If Moira doesn't mind, that is.'

Alex yawned.

'If I'm boring you, please tell me,' Beth half-joked.

'Sorry, there was a call-out last night. A group of four teenagers got lost on Beinn Allighan.'

'Were they alright?'

'One twisted ankle and a nosebleed. They got off lightly. They'd no map or compass between them. Once the path fizzled out, they wandered off the side of the hill. It could've been a lot worse. Bryn searched the old shepherd's hut on a hunch and found them.'

'How's Sarah-Jayne?' Beth asked.

'Can you believe, she's holding down five small gardening jobs now. I was amazed to find out she can tell the difference between a dahlia and a dandelion. She's learning fast.'

'That explains why I haven't seen much of her the last few days. And Tony?'

'Recovered sufficiently to balance on your fence and watch the birds. He's lost a bit of weight too; it's the silver lining to losing one of his nine lives.'

Beth wondered why Alex had really come to see her. He could've texted about the training evenings. She already knew they'd been cancelled so there was no change in the news.

'Look,' she said eventually, 'I'd better get moving. I've got my first night shift at the hospital this evening. I ought to go and get changed.'

'About the other day ... I was a bit harsh on you.'

So that's what this was about. She didn't deserve an apology though. She should never have kept Alex in the dark about what was going on.

'No you weren't. You were quite right. I was wrong to keep Sarah-Jayne's secret from you.'

Alex gave her a long, strange look. Beth couldn't decipher it, but it made her shiver in a pleasant way.

'You have many fine qualities, Beth Hainshaw,' he said in a low, deep voice. Then he leaned down and kissed her.

His lips were warm, dry and firm. Beth kissed him, holding nothing back. They lingered over it, her hands reaching up to touch his hair, to feel its silken strength. A warmth diffused her, spreading over her body. For once in her life, she was utterly and completely in the right place at the right instant.

When they came up for air, Beth had nothing to say. Neither, it seemed, had Alex. Outside, a van drove too fast up the lane. Its brakes screeched as it U-turned at the end and sped off.

'What was that?' Beth said, striving for normality.

'A van?'

'Not *that*. You know what I mean. That. Just then.'

'It was what it was.'

'That's mysterious.'

'Does it have to be boxed up and labelled? Can't we just say that it was right for the moment and leave it at that?'

'Okay, Alex. Let's do that. Now if you'll excuse me, I really do have to get ready for work.' Beth wasn't sure if she was happy or irritated or both or neither. Alex wasn't helping with his obscure answer. Why had he kissed her? *Why had she let him?*

★   ★   ★

Alex went to his office. It was late but that didn't mean the pile of paperwork was any smaller. It was good to work in the silent place when all the traffic was gone and the tourists ensconced in nearby hotels and self-catering cottages.

Why had he kissed Beth? He hadn't planned it. It had felt … *right*. Like coming home. Her lips were soft and her hair delicately scented with violets. He'd felt a surge of protectiveness as he'd held her small frame.

What was that, she'd asked. He had no answer. It was something spontaneous and instinctive. She was annoyed with him for his response, but he'd nothing else to offer. He grinned. She had her prickly moments. She wasn't all sweetness, not all soft like marshmallow. She had backbone and he'd experienced her strong will and courage.

He picked up the top invoice from the bundle and read the figures. For some reason he didn't want to follow his train of thought any longer. But despite that, as he pressed the calculator and totted up the sums, Alex wondered how long Beth would stay in Invermalloch now she was beginning to nurse again. And wondered how that made him feel.

16

'I feel as light as a feather now I don't have to fret about the money, and I've got a treat for you as a thank you,' Sarah-Jayne said with a wide smile.

'It's not me you have to thank, it's Alex,' Beth said honestly. 'He's the one who paid Darren and sorted it all out. All I did was manage to stir things up and make it worse for you. I'm so glad you're out from under Darren's threats now.'

'This treat includes Alex as well. The local Highland Games are on this weekend. I thought we'd go. You and Alex, me and the kids. It'll be a fab day out and Jade needs some fun.'

'Is she okay?'

'She's been having some nightmares since her fall into the ravine. She's quite clingy too and it's been really hard getting her to go to sleep on her own. I've had a few bad dreams myself about losing her

— only in my dreams, she doesn't come back. It's horrible. So …' Sarah-Jayne took a long breath in. 'So I think I'd like it if we all had some fun together. What do you say?'

They were in a tiny cafe on the main street through the village. Beth had worked three nursing shifts by now and was experiencing a mixture of exhilaration at being back at work and exhaustion at the hours it demanded. She liked that she nursed a range of patients and didn't have to focus on any single person. She liked the other staff. She liked the normality of having a job. It was all good, except the shift patterns, which were inevitably at night. That was what happened when you were last in, she told herself. The shifts would improve if she hung on.

She was pleased to see Sarah-Jayne pass by the cafe window and had rapped hard on the glass to get her attention. She hadn't seen her much for a while, nor had she seen Alex. Not since the kiss.

'What exactly is a Highland Games?'

'Oh, I forgot — you've probably never

been to one before, have you.'

'Not a frequent occurrence in London,' Beth said, laughing. 'I'm curious though.'

The waitress arrived, bringing their order. When she'd gone, Sarah-Jayne explained.

'There's one every year. They're popular all over Scotland, mostly in the north of course. It's like a huge gala day. So there's food, music and dance, plus sporting events, like tossing the caber.'

'What on earth is that?'

'It's basically great big men trying to throw tree trunks as far as they can.'

'How can I resist that?' Beth teased. 'Count me in. Um ... will Alex be coming?' she asked casually, putting her plate to one side as the waitress came over to take their tray away.

'I already said so, didn't I? Funny, Alex asked if you'd be going. Have I missed something?'

'No.' Beth said it too quickly and felt the heat rise in her face. Luckily her friend was distracted by some people going past outside the window and failed to notice.

'Oh no, that's Mrs Green from the big house. I hope she doesn't see me. I had a bit of a problem when I was weeding her flowerbeds. I had no idea there were ornamental grasses and that some are quite rare. I thought grass was a weed. I'd better go. Anyway, I'll see you Saturday and we'll have some fun.'

'Bye,' Beth said to Sarah-Jayne's back.

She lingered in the cafe, watching SJ dash up the narrow street in the opposite direction from Mrs Green. Was she ready to see Alex? How should she play it? Should she pretend he never kissed her? Or wait and see how he reacted around her? She got up and paid the bill at the counter. Either way, the weekend was going to be interesting.

* * *

Saturday was dry, with a cut-glass blue sky and a light breeze. There was a sharp scent of late summer to the air and the first birch leaves were turning yellow.

Beth trod on some scattered leaves as she locked up and went next door. The weeks were flying past and she'd promised Milly she'd go and visit her in London. She wasn't looking forward to the long drive south. Nor to leaving what had become a haven, a home, to her. Once she was back in the city she had no doubt her mother would make it hard for her to leave again.

Just a few more weeks, she promised herself. A few weeks to make up her mind about what she wanted. Meanwhile she was standing on Alex's doorstep. Sarah-Jayne had arranged that Alex would give her a lift to the Highland Games, which were taking place in two large fields a half hour north from Invermalloch. She and the kids would meet them there. It made practical sense but Beth had her suspicions that Sarah-Jayne was pushing her and Alex together.

The door opened and Alex came out. He smiled when he saw her and leaned in to kiss her lightly as if it were the most natural thing in the world. So that was the way he was going to play it. She couldn't fight the lilting happiness it gave her. He might not want to discuss what was unfurling between them, but something was. She'd think about it later.

'Are you prepared for the day's delights?' Alex grinned. 'I believe SJ has organised tickets for us to the ceilidh. Got your dancing shoes?'

'Do I need special shoes?' Beth said, trying to ignore the fact that he looked absolutely gorgeous today. His blue cotton shirt matched the deep blue of his eyes and his jaw was freshly shaved. He smelt of soap and spice as he walked beside her to the car. She noticed that his hair was still damp from his shower and it curled a little. He was so much taller than her and his shoulders were broad. With Alex, she felt like nothing bad could happen to her.

'No special shoes required,' he answered her as they drove off. 'Those boots you're wearing will do just fine.'

'Except I don't know any of the highland dance steps.'

Anxiety rose on a small wave inside

her. It was odd how her stress came and went. Some days she believed she was free of it entirely and ready to go back to 'real' life. Then, out of the blue, she'd get that sick, nervous twinge, like now, over a trivial matter. She'd bet no one else was freaking out about the dancing. In fact, they'd be anticipating it with excitement. It was meant to be fun. Only people who'd experienced the draining effects of stress would understand why she felt the way she did.

Then Alex's warm, steady hand descended on hers. The mere touch relaxed her and the anxious knot inside her loosened.

'I'll show you. It's not rocket science and no one expects you to be perfect. That's half the fun of the ceilidh, couples stumbling about copying others. It'll be good.'

'I hope the day lives up to Sarah-Jayne's expectations,' Beth said. 'She's determined that we'll all have fun today. Especially Jade.'

'Poor kid. She's had a delayed reaction

to her ordeal. It's natural and she'll get over it, but it's not easy. But today should be fun. There's plenty of rides for children at the Games, plenty of sweets and burgers to chew on, too.'

* * *

The two fields were busy with white marquees and crowds. The sound of the bagpipes warbled in the air and the smell of hotdogs and candyfloss wafted past Beth's nose. A troupe of highland dancers went past, the girls giggling and chatting loudly. They were dressed in traditional tartan kilts with sashes and black pumps, their hair pulled up tightly into sparkled buns on top of their heads. On a makeshift stage, another group was demonstrating the ancient dances to a haunting melody.

Sarah-Jayne waved them over madly. Beside her, the three children were tucking into sticks of candyfloss the size of their heads. Jade smiled shyly as Beth approached.

'Looking forward to the three-thirty show.' SJ licked her fingers free of candyfloss.

Beth was going to ask what she meant but then everyone was talking at once. Discussing what to do first.

'Sweetie stall,' Jade shouted. 'I'm hungry, so's Peri and Skye.'

'You've just eaten a bag of jellies each and now you've got candyfloss,' Sarah-Jayne said. 'No more until later or you'll make yourselves sick.'

'What about watching the races? There's a two hundred metre run on soon,' Alex suggested. His nieces clamoured to go with their uncle.

Sarah-Jayne wrinkled her nose. 'Not for me, I hate sport. I'm going to have a rummage in the flea market and see if there's any interesting jewellery. Beth? Are you coming with me?'

With an agreement that they'd all meet in a half hour at the ceilidh, Beth followed Sarah-Jayne to the makeshift market under canvas.

As they wandered along a food aisle

with tempting trays of baking and cheeses, meats and local fish, her sixth sense triggered with the sensation that someone was watching her. She looked up. Darren White was at the end of the aisle. He stared at her. Before Beth knew what to do, he'd gone. So quickly, she almost wondered if she'd imagined him there.

The ceilidh was held in the largest marquee. There was a wooden floor and enough space for ten couples at most. A live band was squashed into the corner and the music was loud and impassioned. Alex drew her onto the dance floor. Sarah-Jayne had a partner, an older man who'd asked her to dance.

Alex held her hands in his and the dance began. She had no idea what to do. She looked at the couple in front and tried to imitate their steps. Before long she was laughing at her efforts. No one cared how they danced. She realised that suddenly. Everyone was having fun. With a lightness of heart, she let Alex spin her round in a reel. Her skirts flew out and her hair flicked her face. Her heart pounded with the exercise. The marquee grew hot with all the bodies.

'Like it?' Alex yelled over the commotion.

'I love it,' she shouted back.

She felt the intensity of his grip, the warmth of his body as they danced together. He was a good dancer. He knew the steps. He steered her expertly in a circle on the polished wood.

Her brow was damp with sweat. It was like an aerobic workout. It seemed natural for Alex to escort her to their table and bring her a drink. As if they were a couple. She waited for the inevitable anxiety this thought would bring. Nothing. As if her mind and body agreed. She could get used to this.

'That was fantastic,' Sarah-Jayne said, swallowing a long drink of cranberry juice. 'Anyone for more?'

Beth turned to ask Alex if he'd like to dance another but he wasn't beside her. Thinking he'd gone outside for some fresh air she accepted an offer from a grey-haired man. Several dances later, SJ grabbed her arm.

'Let's go to watch the skydiving. They'll land in the other field. We'd better hurry. Jade, grab Skye's hand. Peri, you are so sticky, no more sweeties for you. I foresee baths in all your futures. Beth? Let's go.'

Sarah-Jayne guided them all over to where a crowd had gathered.

'Where's Alex?'

'He's on the second jump, I think. Or the third. Definitely not the first.'

Beth stared at her. Alex's sister was completely at ease as if nothing was wrong. As if Alex was simply taking a walk on flat ground. And not about to hurl himself out of an aeroplane at ten thousand feet up. Her throat caught with nausea. Any number of things could occur. What if the plane crashed or his parachute didn't open or he landed badly or …

She cupped her hand to her mouth. She was going to be sick. Beside her, Sarah-Jayne and the children were oblivious. They watched skywards as the first tiny figure jumped and came down. No parachute. Beth held her breath. Then, after what felt like an age, a silk blossoming of red as the skydiver's parachute opened. The person floated down to the field to a great roar of applause from the audience.

'Now it'll be Alex,' Sarah-Jayne shouted above the noise.

She had to watch. She was rooted to the spot. Beth's heart rate sped. Her palms were clammy. Alex hadn't told her. Was it deliberate? He must've known she'd freak out. Or maybe he felt she didn't deserve to know. After all, it wasn't as if they were a real couple. She had no hold on him. What had he said at Sarah-Jayne's party all those weeks ago? He had no dependents. He was a free agent and got to choose what he wanted to do with his life.

And he'd chosen this. To indulge in a sport with inherent risks. Just for the adrenaline rush it gave him. No thought of how it felt to watch him. Her mind buzzed with her thoughts. Through it, Sarah-Jayne's raised voice suddenly penetrated.

'Why hasn't he opened his parachute? It ought to be open now. Oh my ... *he's still falling.*'

Sarah-Jayne's face was a mask of horror. Beth risked looking up. Alex was hurtling down. Where was his parachute. What was going on?

Beth ran. She didn't stop to tell SJ. She couldn't face it. She wasn't going to watch Alex die. A meaningless, terrible end. She pushed through the throngs. Happy faces, people eating, little children laughing. It was incongruous.

She made it to the exit. A shuttle bus was bringing and taking people from the event. She got on. She'd no idea where it went. She didn't care. All she needed was to get away. As the bus drove off, Beth put her head on the cold glass window.

It came to her why she cared so much. She was in love with Alex.

17

Alex's feet hit the ground as his knees bent and the landing completed. His reserve parachute had opened shortly after his main had failed and the jump finished to loud applause from the crowd.

He waited for the familiar buzz of adrenaline to hit his nerves. The fantastic wave of life-affirming emotion that made him crave his sports. Yes, it had kicked in. But with a difference. As he gathered up his gear and left the field, Alex relived those moments when his parachute had refused to open.

He had felt no immediate fear. There was confidence that the reserve would act as back up. Yet in those split seconds, instead of sheer headiness amid the freefalling sensation, all the people he cared about had risen up in front of him. *What if...* There it was. What if his reserve failed? What if this was it?

There was no fear for his own life. After all, he'd chosen to do the jump. Instead there was regret that he might not see the people he cared about again. Sarah-Jayne and his three nieces. Andrew. Bryn. Beth. Mostly Beth. They had unfinished business between them. He'd kissed her. She'd quite definitely kissed him back. He found himself wanting to know what would happen next. Surely it wouldn't end on a Highland field? What a stupid way to go.

He was quiet as he made his way to find the others. Sarah-Jayne ran towards him, tears in her eyes.

'Alex! Alex! We thought we'd lost you.' Then suddenly she was hitting his chest with her fists. 'Idiot, why do you do it? Why?'

He gently caught her fists, held them until they stilled and put her arms from him. She let him. The children rushed up. He looked for Beth but she wasn't there.

'Where's Beth?' Alex asked.

'She disappeared,' Sarah-Jayne said. 'I think she's gone home. I don't blame her. I felt sick watching that. Is it worth it, Alex?'

It was a genuine question. He paused before he spoke.

'It used to be.'

Gillian had loved the sport. She'd been the one that initiated them joining a club. Alex had loved the flush to her cheeks and the sparkle in her eyes after a good jump from the aeroplane. She'd revelled in it. Now he wondered if, like Gillian herself, he needed to lay it to rest. After today's event, he didn't think he'd miss the sport. He'd seen the reactions of his family and friends and it wasn't worth it.

It was going to shut another door on his past, he realised. Skydiving was so intensely associated with Gillian in his mind and emotions. He was saying goodbye to another little piece of her. There was sadness, but not the raw agony of even a year ago at this decision. When he conjured Gillian's image, he felt only the sweetness of their young love. It had been untested by time and he'd been guilty of enshrining it at the expense of the years ahead.

'I need to find Beth,' he said. 'Excuse me.'

⋆ ⋆ ⋆

Beth was scrubbing the cottage. She had a mop and a bucket of warm, soapy water. The mop slopped as she pushed it up and down Moira's tiled kitchen floor. If she worked hard enough, she'd keep her thoughts at bay. Except it didn't work. She was in love with Alex. It hadn't gone away. Would never go away. It had crept up on her since the day he'd appeared to fix the dripping tap.

Seeing him falling through the sky like that had made her want to scream. It was beyond terrible. While it had caused that click of recognition that she'd fallen in love with him, it had also caused her fury. A white hot anger that he'd waste his life like that. Without a care for the people who loved him. All on what? A crazy, meaningless activity that gave him a moment's adrenaline surge.

Beth would never forgive him. All

at once she knew she had to leave Invermalloch. There was nothing for her here long term. It hit her with the force of a sledgehammer. She was wasting precious days. Days she could never get back. She was ready for life to begin again. But that life had to be without the man she loved.

The pain of her decision sliced into her. She squeezed her eyes shut until the sensation passed. She gathered up the mop and bucket and stowed them to one side of the kitchen. Her fingers hesitated over the phone. Then she picked up the receiver and dialled.

Moira was delighted to hear from her. She sounded far away over the scratchy line.

'How are you? Do you love my cottage? I knew it would be perfect for you.'

'I do love it,' Beth said, and felt a deep twinge of regret that she had to leave it. 'I'm phoning to say thank you for lending it to me.'

'You're leaving, aren't you? What on earth's happened to make you do so?'

'I'm much recovered and it's time I moved on.'

'Well, I'm glad to hear that. You deserve to be healthy and happy. Are you certain my little sister isn't bullying you to go home?'

Moira was sharp as a tack when it came to Milly.

'It's not that, really, although Mum has tried to persuade me back to London.'

'What then? There's something, I can hear it in your voice. How's Alex, by the way? I asked him to keep an eye on you while you were in the cottage.'

Clearly Moira's sharpness extended beyond her sister, Beth thought wryly. It was just as well she was speaking to her long distance rather than face to face, or her aunt would wring every secret from her.

'He's … he's fine. I've met some lovely people here and I'll be sad to leave them.' Beth choked back a sob before it made a sound down the phone.

'Alex is a gem. He's had a miserable few years by all accounts, losing his fiancée like that. I rather hoped … Well, anyway, you two have met, so that's all I can ask for. If you can get past the bravado with Alex, you won't meet a more loyal soul. But there, I'm wittering on, as elderly aunts tend to do. So, what next for Beth Hainshaw, eh?'

If Moira mentioned Alex once more, Beth was going to burst into tears. She bit her lip. Wasn't falling in love meant to make you happy? Where were the shooting stars, the fireworks, roses and champagne? All she had were tears of misery and a white core of anger at him.

'I don't know.'

'Why don't you stay at the cottage until you do? Jonathan and I won't need it. We're moving on now. San Sebastian is rather nice in the summer but I feel we need a tad more heat in the air now that autumn's not too far away. We've got a place in the Gambia for a few weeks. It's a private game reserve but with a swimming pool and all the little luxuries that Jonathan insists on. In fact, why don't you join us? It'd be super to see you.'

Beth tried to think about going to Africa. It would certainly solve the problem of where to mend her broken heart. Once in the Gambia, she could hardly break her resolve and run back to Invermalloch, not without a lot of money and organisation. Still, she couldn't get there without money either. Agency nursing was paying the bills but she didn't have much put aside. Anyway, she didn't want to go to the Gambia. She'd be playing gooseberry to Moira and Jonathan's on-going love affair. She pinched her nose to stop the tears. Someone else's love affair. Not hers. Was everything from now on going to remind her of Alex?

'Beth, are you still there?'

'Yes. Thanks for the kind invitation but I don't want to intrude. Don't worry about me, I'll decide soon where to go. Maybe I should simply go back to London. At least I've a place to stay there and I did promise Mum I'd visit her soon.'

The prospect held very little joy. But where else should she go? Was she being silly leaving the village so abruptly?

'Alright then. I wish you luck, whatever you do. Remember we'll be back in the UK next spring, so I'll catch up with you then. When you lock up can you please let my handyman know you're going? I'm sure you must've met him by now. Darren will make sure the heating and water are turned off and he'll take care of the keys. You look after yourself, Beth, you hear me now?'

Beth managed a few further words with her favourite aunt and put the phone down. She poured the dirty water from the bucket down the outside drain cover and left the rinsed mop out to dry. The question was, how soon could she leave?

If she packed up quickly, she could drive south overnight and be in England by early morning. The roads would be almost empty at night and if she wanted to, she could stay at a hotel and sleep during the day for a few hours before driving to the far south. The more she mulled it over, the more it appealed.

She didn't want to admit it, but she

knew she was running away. Sarah-Jayne's text had arrived swiftly. *Alex ok. No injuries. Where are u?*

She had no idea how he was okay. The sickening relief mingled with her fury and a sense of helplessness. He was never going to listen to her. He'd never stop doing what he loved.

Suddenly she was running upstairs, grabbing her suitcase from under the bed and stuffing in her clothes. She'd leave notes for Alex and Sarah-Jayne. Although, right now, she'd no idea what she'd write on them.

The doorbell rang as she finished filling her duffel sack with shoes. Her hill walking boots stuck out at the top. She avoided looking at them. Too many associations with this place. As she registered the bell, she heard the door downstairs open. Whoever it was, wasn't waiting for her to answer. She knew who it was.

Alex stood in the hall. Her traitorous heart leapt a beat at the sight of him. He was safe. Not a scratch on him. But there might have been a very different outcome.

She hardened her heart.

'Why did you rush off?' Alex said.

'You know why.' Beth's voice was like ice. She was proud of her control.

'My reserve parachute opened. There was no real danger.'

'No real danger,' she echoed disbelievingly. 'Alex, you could've died today. And for what? A few minutes of … of I don't know what. I don't know why you do it. I guess I'll never know. I'll never understand you.' So much for control. Her body was shaking and her anger had spiralled up like smoke from a raging fire.

'It felt different today. When my parachute didn't open, there was a long moment when I had time to think about things.'

'And?'

'And I thought about you and SJ and the kids. About what a waste it would be if I didn't get down safely.'

'So what are you saying?' She wanted him to spell it out so there could be no mistake.

'I'm saying it'd be a foolish way to go.

That I've got too much at stake to waste it that way.'

'You're not going to skydive any more?' She couldn't hide her relief.

'No, I'm not.'

Beth was ready to move into his arms when he went on, 'I've enough to do with keeping my business going and my climbing.'

He wasn't giving up all risk then. What she was expecting? A miracle?

His gaze flicked to the suitcase standing at the foot of the stairs. He frowned.

'You're leaving?'

'Yes.' Although she was no longer sure. 'Unless you can give me a reason to stay.'

'Beth,' Alex said, and her name on his tongue was soft and full of longing, 'we both know there's something going on between us and I'd like to explore that further, but I don't know what I have to offer you. I told you about Gillian. I'm not sure if there's more of me to give.'

'That's honest, at least,' Beth said. So now she knew that her love for Alex was one-sided. He was warning her off as gently as possible. She swallowed but her throat remained dry as dust. 'I'd like you to leave now.'

When he didn't move, Beth said, 'Please.' The word cracked in half and she didn't trust herself to say more. Instead, she squeezed her eyes shut and prayed he'd be gone when she opened them.

She heard his footsteps and the closing door. Then, and only then, did she allow herself to crumple at the foot of the stairs, head in hands.

18

Her adventure was over. Beth shut and locked End Cottage. Her suitcase and bags were stowed in the boot of the car. Now all she had to do was take the key to Darren White and let him know the cottage was empty. She had washed her face after Alex left, redone her make-up and brushed her hair. No one would guess her inner turmoil. Her heartbreak was hers alone.

She'd thought about phoning her mother to say she was on her way and decided against it. Milly would only fret until she arrived and Beth didn't want the pressure of hurrying her journey along. She'd phone when she was on the outskirts of London. She drove past Sarah-Jayne's farm and slowed. Should she pop in and say goodbye? Her foot pressed on the accelerator and she went past. She couldn't bear to explain to a curious Sarah-Jayne why she was leaving. If she had to say his name, she'd break down all over again.

No, she had to bring on the next phase of her life now. She had to face facts. Falling in love with Alex hadn't worked out. She was on her own. Somehow she had to cope. The first step was to return Moira's keys and then drive south fast, before she changed her mind.

The row of brick buildings where Darren White lived was no more welcoming than her last visit. *With Alex.* When was she going to stop thinking about him? Maybe never. She tilted her chin, pasted a polite smile to her lips and knocked on the door. This wouldn't take long. A quick conversation, pass on the keys and she was out of there.

'What do you want?' Darren said. He glanced beyond her as if looking for someone else. When he saw she was alone, his mood switched as if he was striving to be polite. 'Something wrong at the cottage?'

'So you do maintain it,' Beth said. 'Funny, I haven't seen you there at all since I moved in.'

He shrugged but his gaze was jittery. 'Nothing needed doing. Moira only pays me to fix stuff. You'd have called if there was things going wrong.'

Beth noticed how he kept rubbing his arms as if he was cold. But the day was mild and breezy, no need even for a coat. He didn't seem able to keep still. Now he was making her nervous too. She wanted out of there suddenly.

'Look, I only came to say that I'm leaving. Moira asked me to bring you the keys. She said you'd organise for the heating and the water supply to be turned off. She and Jonathon aren't going to be back until next spring at the earliest. Here.' She thrust the keys at him.

He took them, and his fingers were cold to her touch. She snatched her hand back and stuck it in her dress pocket, rubbing the feel of his skin from hers on the material.

'I'll have to check you've left every-thing in order,' he said. 'Wait 'til I get my jacket.'

'Of course I've left it all in order, it's my aunt's property,' Beth said, rather of-fended. 'You can go and check it yourself, you don't need me there. In fact, I need to go now, I've a long journey ahead.'

'No can do,' Darren shook his head. 'Moira won't be happy if I let you go without checking the house. Wait right there.'

'Oh, for goodness sake,' Beth muttered to his retreating back. 'At least hurry up a bit.'

He came back, dressed in a dark navy felt jacket over his tee-shirt and dirty jeans. Beth felt over-dressed in her wine-coloured jersey dress with her favourite heels.

'We'll take my car,' he said, gesturing to a beat up red Audi.

'I'll follow you back,' Beth said. 'My car's parked over there.'

'It's only a few minutes' drive. Doesn't

make sense to take both cars. Besides, if you're leaving the village for the south, you have to pass this way.'

It made sense, even if she wasn't keen to sit right next to him in his passenger seat.

'Alright,' she nodded. 'This won't take long, will it?'

'That depends.'

She didn't like his sly expression. Did he really think she'd left Moira's cottage in some kind of a state? It was ridiculous. On a wave of irritation she slid into his car. It smelt of old food. Her lovely shoes crunched on greasy pizza boxes and empty coffee takeaway cups. He didn't even apologise for the mess. Didn't appear to notice it or her discomfort.

'You and Alex got it together, eh?' Darren said.

She didn't like his tone. 'That's none of your business.'

'Anything to do with Alex Taylor, I make it my business.'

'What are you talking about?' Beth said, puzzled.

'Alex has it coming, that's what I'm talking about.' Darren's voice was harsher.

Beth's heart thudded. She ought to have taken her own car. The space felt small. The stink of decaying cheese clogged her nostrils. Darren wasn't making any sense. She looked out the car window, searching for End Cottage. Surely they should be there any minute?

'What route are you taking? I don't recognise this,' she said.

'You think I was just going to let him away with all he's done to me?' Darren said, almost conversationally. 'Was that what you thought? What *Alex* thought?'

Now she was afraid. They were nowhere near Moira's cottage. Where was he taking them?

'Please stop the car and let me out,' she said, keeping her voice calm as if nothing was wrong. 'I made a mistake coming with you. I'll walk from here.'

He laughed out loud and shook his head incredulously. 'You think I'm going to let you walk away now?'

Beth's fingers fumbled at the door

lock. It didn't budge. Besides, they were driving fast. Even if she did get it open, there was no way she wanted to jump from the moving car.

'What do you want from me?' To her embarrassment, she heard the panic in her voice. She had to keep it together. Persuade Darren to change the course of his actions. She tried again. 'It's not too late to stop this. Let me out now and I won't mention this to anyone. I promise.'

'Your promise is worth nothing. You're as bad as he is. Alex promised me a place on his team and he lied. Well, now he's going to find out the hard way you don't mess with Darren White.'

'What are you going to do?' Beth asked.

The car swung up a side street and ahead she saw the modern estate of housing come to an end and the wilderness begin.

'I'm going to keep you for a while until Alex learns his lesson.'

'You're kidnapping me?' Beth cried.

'I'm not kidnapping you,' Darren said huffily as if she'd called him a terrible name. 'I'm just taking you away.'

'That's the same as kidnapping; you're holding me against my will.'

'Shut up. You're giving me a headache. I need to think.'

She looked out the window. She needed to track where they were going. She had to be able to find her way back. The problem was, it all looked the same. Marshy grass and bog that rose beyond to the hills and the larger mountains. Here and there a stunted rowan tree which had escaped the grazing sheep. A herd of deer scattered as the car drove past. There was no habitation, not even a railway line or another vehicle on the road. It was a single track that wound in a grey ribbon into the mists of nowhere. Beth wished she'd paid more attention to the lands around the village. But apart from driving to and from the big nearby town she hadn't explored much.

'You were responsible for all of it,' Beth said, ignoring his demand for her to be quiet. 'You cut Alex's rope; you tried to murder him.' Her skin rose up in bumps as she acknowledged what that meant. She was sitting in a car with a man who had tried to kill another human being. What was going to happen to her?

Darren blew out a breath. 'That's crazy talk. I didn't try to kill him. It was a warning, that was all. You should've heard the fuss he made about it. Yeah, you didn't know I was around the Post, did you. I can keep myself out of sight if necessary. No one notices the handyman, unless his job isn't done.'

'You scratched the paintwork on the Land Rovers, you threw the paint at my cottage, burnt the Post and poisoned Alex's cat.'

'Now, wait just a minute,' Darren said. 'Yeah, I scored the Land Rovers. I painted your house red and I enjoyed burning the Post — I only wish it'd burnt right down to the ground. But I never poisoned the cat. Why'd I take it out on a harmless animal? You've got a bad view of me, Beth. I'd like to turn that right around.'

Beth shivered at the silkiness of his last comment. She forced herself not to react. That was what he wanted, wasn't it? To see her squirm in front of him. She wouldn't give him the satisfaction.

'What was it all for?' If she kept him talking, she'd gain a little time to get her brain in gear. She had to work out what to do. What she could do, given her circumstances. She was in a locked car with a madman, driving through the bleakest landscape in the British Isles with no idea of where she was or where she was going.

'To let Alex know what it's like not being in control of what happens. Let him see how he likes it when his world spins away.'

'I don't understand. Why don't you tell me what went on,' Beth said, as if they were having a nice chat over coffee.

Ahead, there was a blot of white against the browns and yellows of the boggy ground. What was it? She gasped as Darren suddenly turned the wheel and the car bumped off the track onto an unsurfaced path. There was a scraping, grinding sound as the car metal met the rushes and mosses and occasional rock.

'It's very simple. I applied to join the Mountain Rescue Team and Alex turned me down. Humiliated me right in front of my girl, Amy. No one does that to me. Doesn't he remember I thrashed him at school? I broke his nose. He wasn't so high and mighty back then.'

Beth didn't believe it. Firstly, Alex had never mentioned Darren applying to join the team. When he and Bryn were trying to work out who was messing with the gear, he'd have certainly put Darren on the list of suspects right there and then. Secondly, Beth didn't believe Alex would humiliate anyone, not even a slug like Darren White.

'Alex never spoke about turning you down.'

'He didn't think I was good enough. He even laughed in my face. Amy dumped me because of it. Well, now he's going to get a taste of his own medicine. I lost Amy, Alex loses you.'

The car gave a final groan and came to rest outside what had been the white blot. Beth saw it was a small house, not more than a couple of rooms. There was a scarred, green, wood door and a tiny window either side. The roof was red corrugated iron with a heavy coating of rust.

'Where are we?' she managed, as Darren got out and pulled open the passenger side door.

'Somewhere nice and far away from Invermalloch and your Alex. No one's going to find you until I want them to.'

'How long are you going to keep me here?' Beth asked, still unable to believe this was happening.

He didn't bother to answer. He pulled her along by her arm. Beth's shoes squelched in the mud. He kicked at the door with his heavy boot. It left a dark scuff mark. Muttering under his breath, he let her go and dug in his jacket pockets. A key jangled as he brought it out. Beth's instinct was to flee. But where? How far was she going to get in her high heels? If only she'd worn her hill walking boots. She saw them in her mind's eye, tucked at the top of her duffel bag. The duffel bag that was right now inside the boot of her car, outside Darren White's home.

'My car is at your house, isn't that a huge giveaway that we met?' she said.

'Well now, thank you for thinking of that,' he smiled coldly. 'Don't you worry about that. When I get back from here, I'll drive it someplace else.'

'You're leaving me here, alone?' Beth said. The thought horrified her.

'I'll be back on and off,' he told her. 'But I can't be seen to disappear right alongside of you, can I? I need to get back and be seen. Besides, I've got work tomorrow. It'll be dark soon and the driving out here isn't good.'

The inside of the building was dark and dank. The floor was made of hardened soil and the only furniture was a rickety table and a bench. Beth was wrong. There weren't two rooms. Only one. A stone fireplace was set in the far wall. It was streaked with soot and a single log was jammed in the hearth. It was not welcoming.

'What is this place?' she whispered.

'Just a place,' he replied unhelpfully.

'They'll be looking for me right now,' Beth said, injecting confidence into her voice.

Darren snickered as if she'd just told the funniest joke ever. 'I don't think so. You must've said your goodbyes already. You told me you were leaving End Cottage. Everyone thinks you've gone back to England. You don't belong up here, do you, Beth? Poor Alex. He'll miss you. What was the plan? Long distance romance. Let me give you a tip, they never work out.' He laughed at his own quip. 'Come along in and sit on the bench. If you're good, I'll make you a fire before I leave.'

'You're seriously going to leave me here on my own? What about food and water? Blankets? It's getting cold.'

It was becoming chilly as the evening drew in. Beth was only in a thin woollen dress. She wished she'd worn a coat. Outside the windows, the sky was a strange pewter shade. As if a storm was brewing.

'Quit moaning,' Darren snapped.

He pushed her hard and she stumbled and sat on the bench. She was afraid of him. There, she admitted it. It was difficult not to show him her fear, but Beth was determined to seem calm. His behaviour was erratic. The jittery movements were back. He rubbed at his arms, flexed up and down on his heels and muttered to himself. Beth sat and waited. Had he planned this? Or was her arrival at his house simply an opportunity not to be wasted?

She longed for Alex. It didn't matter how they'd parted. She needed him. She wanted his arms around her. The comfort of his big body next to hers.

Darren crouched down at the fireplace. She saw an axe next to him. She recognised it. It was the same axe she'd seen him carry out of the outdoor shop the day she'd bought her tent. He turned and saw her look.

'Do you like the irony? I chopped the wood for the fire at the Post with this fine axe. It's an ice axe. Just like the one Alex uses in the winter. Except he gets to use his as part of the team.'

Beth shifted on the bench. The damp was seeping into her thighs through her dress.

'I'm hungry,' she said. 'We've missed dinner.'

'Sorry about that. Tell you what, I'll bring you some crisps tomorrow. That okay?'

There was something chilling about his casual response. He was acting as if all this was normal.

'What am I going to drink tonight? I'm thirsty too.' That was no lie. Her throat was completely parched by her fear.

'I'll swing by with a coke,' he said sarcastically. 'Seriously, Beth, you're starting to annoy me. If I was you, I'd shut right up now before I make you.'

He went back to making a fire. Beth looked about. If he left her locked in the building, she could smash a window out and make a run for it. Where, she didn't know. The land all around was flat and wet and she'd no idea which was north and which was south. Even if she did know, which one should she choose? Or was east or west better? The truth was, she had absolutely no idea. She was city, born and bred. She was far from home. Far from Invermalloch.

'If no one is going to know you've got me, what's the point?' she said.

'What?' He sounded exasperated. His hands were black with ashes from the remains of the last fire.

She wanted him to make a proper fire. Her fingers and toes were numb with the increasingly cold air. But she also wanted to understand what his plan was. That way, she hoped to calculate when he'd be back for her. If he was coming back.

'You said no one was going to be looking for me because I'd said my goodbyes. That they'd think I was on my way to London by now.'

'Yes.'

'So what's the point of bringing me here? How's that going to teach Alex a lesson?'

A dreadful idea hit her. Please God, no. Surely Darren wasn't going to wait until

Alex started to wonder why he'd failed to hear from her? That could take days. Weeks. Alex wouldn't expect a phone call until she got to London, and perhaps not even then, considering how they'd left things.

'Because I'm going to send him an anonymous letter, that's how. Get him to cough up some cash for your safe return.'

'He's never going to give you ransom money.' Beth shook her head. It was far-fetched. Darren had clearly watched too many movies.

'He will. If he wants your safe return. Then, while he's finding you, I'm going to be safely on my way with Amy on a one-way ticket to somewhere hot with no extradition agreement with the UK.'

'Right.' Beth smiled as if it all made total sense. He'd lost it entirely. There was an unfocussed quality to his eyes.

'You don't get it do you? I'm not playing a game. This is real. Get used to this, you might be here longer than you'd like.'

He leaned right down to her and Beth shied away. He smelt. Of sweat and tension, and, weirdly, of mothballs. Maybe it was his old jacket. Pulled out of a musty wardrobe in his house.

He grabbed her hands and bound them with twine. Tightly. The rough, thick string scratched her painfully. Her knuckles throbbed. It felt like her blood supply was being cut off to her fingers.

'Sorry. Can't have you escaping. Although …' He made a show of looking out of the grimy window, and grinned at her. 'Don't know where you'd go in any case. There's a lot of blanket bog out there. Did you know some of it is metres deep with just a scab of moss on it? If you step in the wrong place you can go straight through. Not a nice way to drown, in peat water.'

Beth opened her mouth but he shushed her with a motion of his palm.

'I know what you're going to say. That I'll never get away with this. But the thing is, Beth, I will get away with it. You'd better hope so. I'll be rich and I'll have Amy back with me. She likes spending money. You and old Alex get each other.

If he finds you, of course. Anyway, I've got to go. I'll see you tomorrow.'

It was on the tip of her tongue to shout 'don't go'. Even Darren's company was better than being left alone here. He shut the door and the blast of air lifted soot from the burning log. She coughed. Once the car engine had gone, the place was silent. A breeze rattled the windows, making her feel more isolated. She shivered violently. She was tied up in an abandoned building somewhere in the middle of the bog lands. What was she going to do now?

19

He'd lost her for good. And it was all his own fault. Alex paced his home like a captive tiger. She'd told him to leave and he had. Then he'd had to listen to her locking up End Cottage and driving off. Forever. It was getting his head round that which hurt. She wasn't coming back to Invermalloch. Right now, she'd be driving south on the main road. She'd hit the English border in the small hours of darkness. Gone.

And he'd let her go. He was angry with himself for handling it so badly. But he was also angry with Beth. She hadn't given them a chance. All he'd asked for was time to work out what was going on between them. She obviously didn't think it worth waiting for.

He strode upstairs. His study was a refuge. Always had been. Yet as he stood there, he didn't feel its calming effect.

Tony was asleep on the desk chair, his favourite spot. The wood clad walls failed to warm him. The photographs covering them, his best memories, were a blur. All he saw in his mind's eye was Beth.

He was attracted to her. A magnetic desire that increased the more he was with her. Her dark hair and expressive eyes, her scent and the softness of her lips when he'd kissed her. But more than that, he was drawn to her qualities. She was brave and determined and ready to overcome any obstacle with a fierce will. She hadn't hesitated the day Jade was in danger. Despite her own fears about taking risks, she'd risked all to help SJ's little girl.

She knew how to enjoy the peace of small moments too. He thought about her watching the garden birds from her kitchen. The shape of her face in repose, utterly at peace with life. He envied her. He hadn't fully understood that until now. He wanted — *needed* — to spend those moments with her. Fully connected in spirit. He got it. Finally he got what she was talking about. Simply being together was enough. They didn't need high adventure to feel the intensity of being together.

There was an itch at the back of Alex's brain. A thought that wouldn't quite arrive. He glanced at his watch. Was it too late? Should he drive after her and beg for one more chance? He picked up his mobile and set it down. She wouldn't answer her phone if she was driving.

He went back to pacing, much to Tony's disgust. The big cat jumped off the chair and stalked out of the room. Too much noise and activity. The itch grew in his head. What was evading him? He stopped in front of Gillian's photograph. He'd used her name as a barrier to what Beth was telling him.

She wanted a reason to stay. He'd been put on the spot. As if a sharp, bright light had been shone right at him. She had wanted him to tell her how he felt. So he'd used Gillian in defence. A stalling technique because he hadn't felt ready to strip his emotions bare. *I'm not sure there's more of me to give.* What a lie. What he felt for Beth was a never-ending longing. Shot straight from the heart.

He was getting to it. The itch had reached his forehead. Alex knew it. He was about to say it right out loud when the door to his house burst open and he heard Bryn shout. At the same moment, his phone buzzed on the desk as a text came in. He picked it up and everything shattered.

★   ★   ★

The fire had gone out. There were only smoking embers that gave off no heat. Beth's hands throbbed. Her wrists were sore from the twine, and her ankles too. She shivered. The wool of her dress was too thin to give any protection from the icy room. Her toes were like blocks of ice. She wished again she hadn't worn such flimsy footwear. Not that she could've foreseen how her day would end.

She tried to calculate how long it had been since Darren left. She hadn't dared to move from the damp bench in case he came back and found her trying to escape. She listened. It was eerily silent apart from the soughing wind which shook the building. No sound of a car motor or of someone in the vicinity.

What would Alex do in these circumstances? Thinking about him, Beth felt stronger. More determined to fight her way out of this. Because she'd realised something. She was deeply and irreversibly in love with Alex Taylor. But she hadn't told him. She'd wanted him to say it to her first. When he hadn't, she'd been a coward and run away. Now she wanted a chance to tell him. Whether he loved her back or not, it didn't matter. Beth didn't care. She just needed to say the words to him. She loved him with all her heart.

She wished for his strength, for his lack of fear, for his confidence in the abilities of his own body. All these qualities were what would get her through this situation. She had to draw on all her reserves. She had to think what Alex would do.

Beth cast around her. It was gloomy in the dank space. The only light was the moonlight shining in the dirty windows. Apart from the papery disc of the moon, it was dusky grey and getting darker out there. A huge part of her desired to stay in the building. A smaller part knew she had to leave. Darren would be back the next day. She had no idea what kind of mood he'd be in or whether he'd have changed his views on her fate.

The moonlight glittered on a small box by the fireplace. Beth frowned. She squinted at it. No way. Was it possible? Then she laughed right out loud. It was Darren's cell phone. It must have fallen out of his jacket pocket as he crouched down to make the fire. Her own phone was safely tucked inside her handbag, which was on the passenger seat of her car. She had no idea where her car was now. Where Darren had driven it to.

The question was, could she reach his phone? Her delight faded as she followed the implications. It wasn't going to take Darren long to realise he'd lost his phone and where. When he did, surely he'd be back here to get it. Beth's time was running out.

She lifted her wrists in despair. He tied them together, and just as she'd hoped he'd leave her feet free, he'd grabbed her ankles and bound them too. Even when he was doing so, Beth thought there was something slightly pathetic about him. She was frightened of him because he was unpredictable. But everything he did had a whiff of bad movies about it. As if he'd seen all these actions on a screen and was mimicking them.

No wonder Alex had been puzzled by the vandalism. It had gone from a deadly cut to his climbing rope to small, petty actions, and then crescendoed to a potentially fatal act of arson. Darren didn't seem to understand the results of his action. He'd only nicked the rope as a warning. He'd liked the fire because it would destroy the Post. He hadn't thought of human casualties. He was offended that she believed he'd hurt an animal.

He really was pathetic. What kind of master criminal dropped their phone right where their victim could reach it? Beth's glee made her wriggle. Her wrists slid at the movement. There was some give to the twine. She put her teeth to the knot and pulled.

Eventually, when her teeth were so painful she wanted to scream, the knot gave. She shook her hands free and bent to untie her feet. The blood rushed back into her extremities and she gasped. Then she was reaching for the cell phone.

She paused. The air clung to her, moist and cold. A stink of ashes and diesel oil and dirt from the floor wafted. Outside, the wind made the iron roof rattle and clash. It was a noise without hope. It signalled the bleak lands beyond. Beth shivered. Miles of blanket bog surrounded her. Peat and moss and dark waters she could vanish inside and never be found. But what was the alternative? She looked at the phone and pressed the button.

★　★　★

The itch had exploded into one overriding truth. Alex was in love with Beth. Maybe he'd loved her ever since their midsummer camp. The moment when she rose from the sea like a mermaid. Or when her hair was wild from the breeze as they ate breakfast together in front of their tents. Whatever the case, he needed to be with her right now to tell her how he felt. He needed to kiss her until their souls mingled.

But she was missing. Bryn had been lucky to catch a brief glimpse of her in a car with Darren White driving too fast through the village. He'd gone immediately to Alex, his gut instinct telling him that something was wrong. Then somehow, miraculously, Beth had managed to send a text to him.

He had to find her. She was out there on a blasted dark moor with no equipment, no compass and no idea where she was going. All she knew was she had to flee. Alex turned to Bryn's concerned face. He was waiting for him to make a decision.

'I have to call this in,' he said. 'We have to get the team assembled. The only problem is where we narrow down the search area to. All we know is that they were headed north. Every minute Beth's out there she's in danger. We could be hours from finding her.'

'Can the police track the signal from the cell phone she's using?' Bryn said.

'I've no idea. The signal didn't last. I tried to phone her back but it was dead. You know how patchy mobile phone reception is out between the mountains. The only way we can find Beth is if we find Darren.'

'The police are already looking for him,' Bryn said. 'I phoned them before we came over. Let's get the team and get out there.'

Alex's front door burst open again and he wondered how long the hinges would last. Sarah-Jayne came in on a rush of night air. Her curls sprang from her head in all directions and she was wearing an apron stained with orange food splashes.

'I came as soon as I got your call. I

can't believe it. Is Beth really missing?' There were tears in Sarah-Jayne's eyes.

Alex shushed her. 'Bryn and I need to get going. You stay here until we send you news. Beth might try to phone here.'

'The guys are ready to go,' Bryn said, snapping his radio off. 'We'll rendezvous at the north exit of the village and decide where to go from there.'

Alex and Bryn exchanged worried glances. They both knew the team could be searching for days on the bog terrain and not find Beth. There were hundreds of miles of nothing between Invermalloch and any large town.

'Wait — he must have taken Beth to Canaich,' said Sarah-Jayne

'What did you say?' Alex grabbed her and his sister froze.

'You said the north exit? Well, I'm guessing that's where they are, then.' Sarah-Jayne rubbed her nose on her sleeve. 'After all, what else is along that north road that Darren knows well?'

'Okay, okay,' Alex waved her words away impatiently. 'What is Canaich?'

'It's an old shepherd's hut, it belongs to Amy. Actually it was Amy's grandfather's home. He was a shepherd for the Laird way back and ...'

But Alex hadn't waited to hear any more. He and Bryn raced to the Land Rover, Bryn's radio to his mouth relaying the location to the rest of the team. As he spun the steering wheel and they went to initiate the rescue, Alex's heart pounded. Where was Beth? And would he find her in time?

★ ★ ★

Beth had never felt so alone. The only thing keeping her going now was Alex. She had to see him. She had to hold him tightly and never let go. All the issues and differences between them meant nothing. If he found her, she'd never begrudge him his passion for the hills. Somehow they'd find a way to work it all out between them.

She had to accept that he loved Gillian. What she wanted to discover was whether there was room for him to love another. If she stayed, if she gave them a chance to grow together. Beth wished for that opportunity desperately. Her legs were numb from the icy water and slick with peat. She was walking on the bog. Terrified it'd give way beneath her.

The building was out of sight. At least Darren couldn't find her. Not in this awful place. The worry was, could Alex? He must've called in the Mountain Rescue Team by now. Assuming he had got her text. She had to have faith they'd find her. She had to keep going.

The wind whipped up her hair and made her wet dress cling to her. She was shivering uncontrollably. Now Beth worried about hypothermia. She had a screaming thirst but was afraid to drink the peaty water under her feet. She had a long cut on her calf where her skin had scraped on a branch.

It was shocking how quickly civilisation disappeared. She was without shelter, sufficient warm clothing and had no food or water. How long would she last? Only her wish for Alex kept her going. She had to prove to him she could make it. She laughed but it came out sounding like a sob. Risk-averse Beth Hainshaw, wading in bog water up to her knees, the wind beating on her and a madman possibly behind her somewhere. If she survived this, she'd never feel anxiety over everyday life again, she vowed.

She sank down for a short rest. With a jolt, she opened her eyes. She'd fallen asleep. There were voices, shouting. She pushed herself up unsteadily. There were lights bobbing in the distance. Men's voices.

'Alex,' she shouted. 'Alex!'

⋆ ⋆ ⋆

Huddled in a blanket on the back seat of the Land Rover, Beth was reminded of Jade's rescue. Around her, the team were busy and the radios squawked as the stand down was relayed. The police had gone. Alex brought over a towel. Beth's legs were stained dark brown with the peat. One shoe was missing. The other, sadly, was destined for the rubbish bin.

'What's going to happen to Darren?' Beth asked.

'He'll be having a long conversation with our police colleagues,' Alex said, drily.

'I feel sorry for him,' Beth said. 'I think he's ill rather than evil.'

'Don't waste your thoughts on him. You could've had a very different end to today, thanks to Darren.' Alex's mouth set grimly.

'He said he wanted you to suffer like he had,' Beth said, unable to give it up while it still niggled. She had to understand the nightmare she'd been through before she could stop thinking about the man who'd kidnapped her.

'He claims I turned him down for the team. But he never applied to join. Was that all in his head?' Alex frowned.

'Try to remember,' Beth urged. 'He must've given some indication he'd like to join.'

'There was one incident, but I honestly

thought he was joking.'

'What was a joke to you obviously was deadly serious to him.'

'I wish I'd realised that.'

'He said you'd humiliated him in front of Amy. She'd dumped him because he didn't get into the team, or so he says. I suspect, from other comments he made, that Amy likes a guy with cash and he didn't always have enough to keep her in the style she liked. That fits with him bullying Sarah-Jayne for the money she owed him. She told me that as a couple they were very volatile, splitting up and getting back together. They'd had a big blow up before I arrived in the village. Does that fit with this incident you mentioned?'

Alex sighed. 'It was trivial. At least to me. It was a day in the spring when I was cleaning out the Post. Darren was meant to be working there, fixing a window frame that had busted. Then Amy turned up and there wasn't much work going on. He drifted over to where I was clearing up and threw in a comment about having skills I'd be mad not to take onto the team. Darren has absolutely no relevant mountaineering experience; it was clearly an empty boast for Amy's benefit. It riled me. Maybe it was foolish but we'd had a few recent rescues and I guess I was comparing him to the real heroes in our team who put their lives on the line day after day to bring people home safe. I laughed at him, treated it as a joke. Then I forgot all about it. Until now.'

'You're right,' Beth said, 'I don't want to waste another second on Darren or Amy. I want to talk about us, Alex. If there is an us.' She lifted her eyes to his. What she saw there made her shiver — but not with cold.

'I was a fool to let you go,' Alex said. 'I should have told you how I feel about you, but I was terrified.'

'Alex Taylor, mountain man — terrified?' Beth teased gently.

'Yep.'

Then he pulled her close and told her with his mouth exactly how he felt about her.

'I don't want to change you,' Beth said,

when they came up for air. 'If it wasn't for your experience and skills, I wouldn't be sitting here right now. I love you, the whole of you, for who you are.'

'I can manage a little change.' Alex kissed her, just to remind himself how wonderful it felt. 'I'd like to sit with you at your kitchen window and watch the birds. I want to grow old with you, Beth.'

'I want that too, but not just yet. We've got plenty of years together. I want to share lots of experiences with you, make our memories good ones.'

'Beth Hainshaw, will you marry me?'

'Mmmm, kiss me again and then I'll answer you.'

We do hope that you have enjoyed reading this large print book.

Did you know that all of our titles are available for purchase?

We publish a wide range of high quality large print books including: **Romances, Mysteries, Classics General Fiction Non Fiction and Westerns**

Special interest titles available in large print are: **The Little Oxford Dictionary Music Book, Song Book Hymn Book, Service Book**

Also available from us courtesy of Oxford University Press: **Young Readers' Dictionary (large print edition) Young Readers' Thesaurus (large print edition)**

For further information or a free brochure, please contact us at: **Ulverscroft Large Print Books Ltd., The Green, Bradgate Road, Anstey, Leicester, LE7 7FU, England. Tel:** (00 44) **0116 236 4325 Fax:** (00 44) **0116 234 0205**

PALACE OF DECEPTION

Helena Fairfax

When a Mediterranean princess disappears with just weeks to go before her investiture, Lizzie Smith takes on the acting role of her life — she is to impersonate Princess Charlotte so that the ceremony can go ahead. As Lizzie immerses herself in preparation, her only confidante is Léon, her quiet bodyguard. In the glamorous setting of the Palace of Montverrier, Lizzie begins to fall for Léon. But what secrets is he keeping from her? And who can she really trust?